Copyright © 2025 Firen Media Corporation

ISBN: 9798298277006

All rights reserved. No part of this book may be reproduced in any manner whatsoever without written permission except in the case of brief quotations embodied in critical articles and reviews.
First Printing, 2025

FIREN

From Male Ruling to Female Ruling

Linda Lee Kelly

Firen Media Corporation Limited

"I have trouble falling asleep. One night at 4am, I still couldn't sleep. I heard a voice in my head saying that I have to write it down or I would go insane. And so, I surrendered to the muse. Isolated myself for many sleepless nights and put those thoughts in words. Once they were out, I hardly recognized it as my own writing."
By Linda Lee Kelly

CONTENTS

Copyright
Title Page
Epigraph
Dedication
Chapter 1: The Mailroom Girl — 1
Chapter 2: Shining Nails — 15
Chapter 3: Firen — 23
Chapter 4: Easy Day of Work — 29
Chapter 5: Beekwomen Hotel — 35
Chapter 6: Catering Staff — 58
Chapter 7: Dada for Dada — 74
Chapter 8: Strange Phone Call — 84
Chapter 9: Shadows in the Night — 92
Chapter 10: A Short Notice — 102
Chapter 11: An Invitation — 116
Chapter 12: A Business Trip — 126
Chapter 13: Short Fingers — 140
Chapter 14: The King's Gambit — 147
Chapter 15: Crocodile's Tear — 156
Chapter 16: Mirage and Miracles — 173
Chapter 17: Shadow of A Queen — 198

Attributes to my loved ones who would like to stay anonymous.

CHAPTER 1: THE MAILROOM GIRL

At 30 years old, Clara had always imagined her life would look… well, *different*. She had dreamed of so much more—of stepping into a sleek, high-rise office, the kind with floor-to-ceiling windows that framed a glittering city skyline. She had pictured herself in tailored blazers and sharp heels, her voice steady and commanding as she led meetings, made decisions, and left her mark on the world. She had envisioned climbing the corporate ladder with purpose, each promotion a hard-earned victory, each milestone a step closer to the life she had always wanted. Her desk would be a reflection of her success: clean, organized, with just a few personal touches—a framed photo of her standing atop a mountain she'd summited, a small potted plant she somehow managed to keep alive, and maybe a coffee mug that said something clever like *"Boss Lady."*

But reality? Reality had a way of humbling even the most determined dreamers. Instead of that corner office, Clara found herself in a modest mailroom, its fluorescent lights casting a dull glow over stacks of packages and dusty shelves. Her "desk" was a cramped workstation, cluttered with sticky notes and half-empty pens. Her days were spent sorting mail, fielding last-minute requests, and trying to keep up with the endless stream of deliveries. It wasn't glamorous. It wasn't impactful. And it certainly wasn't what she had envisioned for herself at 30.

Two years had slipped by, and Clara felt like she was drowning in an ocean of routine, struggling to keep her head above water.

Every day was the same—a blur of sorting endless stacks of mail, delivering packages to people who barely acknowledged her presence, and wrestling with the temperamental office printer that jammed more often than it worked. She had once clung to the hope that this job would be a stepping stone, a way to inch closer to something better, something meaningful. But now, that hope felt like a cruel joke. The door to opportunity wasn't just closed; it was locked, bolted, and guarded by people who never seemed to notice her, let alone offer her a key. Each passing day chipped away at her spirit, leaving her wondering if she was destined to be invisible forever.

The office was a relentless sea of men in crisp, tailored suits, their laughter and self-assured voices filling every corner of the room as they tossed around words like *mergers*, *acquisitions*, and *market dominance*—as if they were kings shaping the world. Clara moved through it like a ghost, unseen and unheard, except for the moments that made her skin crawl—the lingering stares that felt like they were peeling away her dignity, the offhand remarks about her looks, spoken with an ease that made it clear they never considered how they might make her feel. It was as if she existed only in the spaces between their conversations, acknowledged only when her presence could serve their egos, their fleeting amusement. And no matter how hard she worked, how much effort she put in, she couldn't shake the sinking feeling that to them, she was nothing more than background noise.

One especially frustrating afternoon, Clara found herself clutching a heavy stack of documents as she rode the elevator to the 15th floor, her fingers tightening around the pages as if bracing for battle. The doors slid open, and almost instantly, laughter erupted from the nearby break room—deep, confident, unbothered. She wasn't trying to eavesdrop, but their voices carried, filling the hallway with talk of golf swings, luxury watches, and then—her stomach twisted—something about "*the mailroom girl.*"

Heat surged to her cheeks before she even processed the words. She didn't want to know what they were saying. She didn't want to hear the punchline. But the knowing chuckles, the easy, careless way they spoke, told her everything. She lowered her head, quickening her pace, her heart hammering with humiliation. Dropping the documents onto the nearest desk, she turned on her heel, barely breathing until she was back in the safety of the mailroom—her tiny, windowless refuge. There, with the hum of the fluorescent lights overhead, she let out a shaky breath, swallowing the lump in her throat. It didn't matter how hard she worked or how invisible she tried to be. To them, she was nothing more than a passing joke.

Back in her cramped, cluttered workspace, Clara slumped into her chair, exhaling a breath that felt heavier than it should. The room was dim, the walls scuffed and peeling, as if they, too, had grown tired of being overlooked. She traced a crack in the paint with her eyes, wondering how much longer she could keep doing this—keep being invisible, keep swallowing her frustration, keep pretending it didn't sting when the men in the office treated her like a tool to be used when convenient and discarded the moment she wasn't needed.

She was exhausted. Exhausted from the lingering stares, the offhand comments, the way her name was barely remembered unless it was attached to a request or a joke at her expense. Tired of being reduced to a fleeting amusement, a decorative afterthought in a world where her work, her ambition, *she*— none of it seemed to matter.

The only person who ever seemed to truly *see* her was Evelyn, who was a project manager working on the same floor, and was the only female manger at her level in this location. At 35, no husband, no kids, Evelyn had weathered more than a decade in this place, rising through the ranks with a sharp mind and an unwavering confidence that Clara envied. She was bold, unafraid to speak her mind, and unwilling to shrink herself to make others comfortable. And yet, even Evelyn wasn't untouchable.

Clara had seen the way men dismissed her ideas in meetings, how they spoke over her, how they treated her success as an exception rather than proof that she belonged. If Evelyn still had to fight to be taken seriously, what chance did Clara have? The thought settled in her chest like a weight, pressing down on the last bit of hope she had left.

One day, Evelyn lingered in the mailroom longer than usual, her usual sharp posture softened by something heavier—exhaustion, frustration, maybe both. She leaned against the counter, arms crossed tightly over her chest, and let out a long, tired sigh.

"Sometimes I wonder why I even bother," she muttered, her voice laced with resentment. "These men act like they own the place, like we're just here to make them look good."

Clara looked up, startled by Evelyn's unguarded honesty. She had always admired her for being fearless, for speaking her mind. But hearing that even she felt worn down by it all made Clara's own frustration feel more real—more justified.

"I know what you mean," Clara said, her voice quieter, almost hesitant. "It's like no matter how hard I work, I'm just 'the mailroom girl.' They don't see me as anything more than that."

Evelyn studied her for a moment before nodding, her expression softening with something close to understanding.

"It's exhausting, isn't it?" she said. "Constantly having to prove yourself, only to be ignored, dismissed, or treated like a joke. It wears you down." She exhaled sharply and then met Clara's gaze, her voice gentler now. "But don't let them break you. You're smarter and more capable than they'll ever bother to notice. And one day, when they finally do—when they realize what you were worth all along—it'll be too late for them."

Clara swallowed the lump in her throat, holding onto Evelyn's words like a lifeline. Maybe she *was* more than just the mailroom girl. Maybe, one day, she'd prove it.

Her words struck a chord with Clara. For the first time in a long while, she felt seen—not as the mailroom girl, but as a person with potential. Evelyn's encouragement sparked something in her.

As Clara sat in the mailroom, staring at the peeling paint on the walls, her mind drifted back to her childhood in a small town in Northern Alberta. It was the 1990s, and life moved at a slower pace there. The winters were long and harsh, the kind that made you appreciate the warmth of a crackling fire. Her parents were elementary school teachers, both strict and hardworking, had always emphasized the importance of education. They believed it was the key to a better life, a way to escape the limitations of their small town.

Clara could still see it—the worn wooden kitchen table, its surface etched with years of scribbled notes and late-night studying. She remembered the dim glow of the overhead light, the way it flickered slightly, casting shadows over her textbooks. And she remembered her father, standing behind her, his presence heavy with expectation.

"You have to be better, Clara," he would say, his voice firm but never cruel. "The world won't hand you anything. You have to earn it."

She would nod, gripping her pencil tighter, the weight of his words settling deep into her bones. Failure was never an option, not in their house. Not when so much was riding on her success.

Her mother, just as determined, would sweep in from the kitchen, drying her hands on a dish towel before resting a gentle but steady hand on Clara's shoulder. "Education is your ticket out of here," she would remind her, her voice softer but no less urgent. "Don't waste it."

Clara carried those words with her like a weight, a constant reminder that she had to prove herself. They pushed her to excel in school, to pour every ounce of her energy into her studies. She had always been a dreamer, her heart brimming with curiosity and a deep love for stories and art. History captivated her—not just as a subject, but as a tapestry of lives woven across time and space, connecting her to something greater. And then there was painting, her sanctuary. With each stroke of the brush, she could lose herself in the swirl of colors, the canvas becoming a world where she felt most alive.

Clara still remembered the day she walked across the stage at the University of Alberta, her degrees in History and Fine Art clutched tightly in her hands. Her parents had beamed with pride from the audience—but even then, she had seen the flicker of worry in her father's eyes.

"What will you do with those degrees?" he had asked later, his voice gentle but lined with concern. "You need something practical, Clara."

She had loved her father dearly, but those words had stung. Because what he really meant was: Dreams don't pay the bills.

And in many ways, he was right.

The job market had been brutal. Employers wanted accountants, engineers, tech specialists—not dreamers who could recite Renaissance art movements or debate medieval trade routes. Her résumé, polished and hopeful, was met with polite rejections or, worse, silence.

So, she took the only job she could find: catering.

It was grueling work—long hours on her feet, her hands raw from scrubbing dishes, her back aching from hauling trays. At night, she would collapse onto her tiny apartment couch, too exhausted to paint, too drained to even think. Somewhere along the way, the vibrant, ambitious woman she had been at graduation began to fade.

But Clara had never been one to surrender quietly. Late at night, when the world was still, she would drag herself to her easel and paint. Not for money. Not for recognition. But because she had to—because without it, she feared she might disappear entirely.

Her parents, ever practical, gently nudged her toward teaching. "You could come home," her mother had said. "The high school also needs an art teacher." And for a moment, Clara had considered it.

Home was safe. Familiar. It was Sunday dinners at her parents' table, and running into childhood friends at the grocery store, and knowing every street corner by heart. But it was also… small. Too small for the dreams that still burned inside her. She wanted more. More than her hometown could offer. More than catering. More than settling.

She wanted **New York.**

The city had called to her for years—a place where art wasn't just admired but *lived,* where every street corner pulsed with energy, where possibility hung in the air like the scent of rain before a storm.

And then, in the cruelest twist of fate, the decision was made for her.

One ordinary evening, while daydreaming over a tray of canapés at a local dinner event, her phone rang.

A car accident. Her parents. Gone.

The grief nearly destroyed her. For weeks, she drowned in it—lost in a haze of cheap wine and sleepless nights, curled on her couch in the same clothes for days, the walls of her apartment closing in around her.

Until one morning, she woke from a dream. In it, she was a child again, wobbling on her bike as her father steadied her. "Try again," he had said, smiling as she fell. "You'll get it."

When she opened her eyes, something inside her had shifted. She stood in front of her mirror, hollow-eyed and disheveled—and made a decision. It's time to go.

Two weeks later, she was on a plane to New York with nothing but a suitcase and a heart full of hope.

However, the city did not welcome her with open arms. It was louder, dirtier, and far more ruthless than she had imagined. The skyscrapers didn't glitter—they loomed. The people didn't smile—they shoved past her on the sidewalk, eyes fixed on their own destinations.

And the art world? It didn't care about her degrees. Or her dreams.

Clara had expected struggle. But this—this was something else entirely. Yet somewhere beneath the fear and the loneliness, that same stubborn spark still flickered. The one that had kept her painting late at night when the world told her to give up.

New York hadn't broken her yet. And she refused to let it.

Her job search became a relentless cycle of hope and disappointment, a rollercoaster that left her emotionally drained. Each application she sent out was a tiny beacon of hope, a whispered prayer that maybe, just maybe, this would be the one. But interviews—her Achilles' heel—left her flustered and self-conscious. No matter how much she prepared, her thoughtful answers would falter under the weight of the interviewer's gaze. Her quiet demeanor, which she had always seen as a strength, was mistaken for disinterest or lack of passion.

The rejections piled up, each one a sharp blow to her confidence. "We've decided to move forward with another candidate," they would say, their words polite but cutting. And worse still, most of the time, her meticulously crafted resume disappeared into the void, never earning so much as a callback.

Clara felt invisible, her qualifications and diligence overshadowed by the sheer competitiveness of the job market. She would lie awake at night, staring at the ceiling of her tiny apartment, wondering if she had made a mistake. Was she fooling herself, chasing a dream that was never meant to be hers? The doubt crept in, whispering cruel truths she tried to ignore. But even in her darkest moments, she clung to a fragile thread of hope—the belief that one day, someone would see beyond her nerves, beyond her quiet exterior, and recognize the potential that burned within her.

In the meantime, she had to survive.

Clara eventually landed a job in the mailroom of a financial firm, a far cry from the career she had envisioned. It was mundane work, sorting and delivering envelopes, running errands for people who barely noticed her existence. But it paid the bills, and for now, that was necessary.

As Clara sat in the quiet mailroom, surrounded by stacks of forgotten envelopes and half-empty coffee cups, she let her mind drift back to the path that had led her here. It had been anything but easy. The strict upbringing, the grueling hours spent buried in textbooks, the relentless pressure to succeed—it had all been for *something*, hadn't it? She had believed that if she worked hard enough, sacrificed enough, she would carve out a life that made her parents proud.

Her chest tightened as she pictured them, their expectant faces, the weight of their sacrifices pressing against her ribs. They had given up so much to give her a chance at something *better*. And now? Now she was delivering packages, sorting mail, and fixing jammed printers in a city that barely noticed she existed.

Would they be disappointed if they saw her now? Would they wonder if all those years of pushing her to be the best had been wasted? Or would they understand—that this was just a step, not the destination? That she was still *trying*?

She wanted to believe they would. That they would see beyond the fluorescent-lit mailroom and the title that meant nothing. That they would see *her*—fighting, enduring, refusing to give up. But doubt lingered like a shadow, whispering that maybe, just maybe, she wasn't moving forward at all.

Her thoughts were abruptly interrupted by the sharp voice of a senior manager. "Clara, I need this package sent out ASAP," he said, dropping a bulky envelope on her desk without waiting for a response. She nodded, pushing her memories aside, and got to work. The mailroom was a flurry of activity as she organized the outgoing packages, ensuring everything was labeled correctly and ready for pickup.

By the time the delivery guys arrived, Clara was exhausted but relieved. She handed over the last of the mail, double-checked her work, and finally clocked out for the day. The office was quiet now, the hum of the printer replaced by the faint echo of her footsteps as she made her way to the elevator.

As she stepped out into the crisp evening air, Clara felt the weight of the day lift slightly. The city lights sparkled around her, a reminder of why she had come here in the first place. She walked towards the subway station, her mind drifting back to her small rental condo in New Jersey. It wasn't much—just a modest space with a view of the Hudson River—but it was her space. A place where she could unwind, paint, and dream about what might come next.

Clara was lost in thought as she wandered through the bustling streets of New York City, her mind a whirlwind of reflections and daydreams. The city's noise faded into a distant hum as she replayed conversations, pondered her future, and imagined scenarios that might never come to pass. Her steps were slow and deliberate, her gaze fixed on the pavement, unaware of her surroundings.

As Clara turned the corner, lost in her thoughts, her shoulder collided with someone standing by the curb. A cigarette dangled lazily from his lips, and the sharp scent of tobacco stung her nose. Before she could even register what had happened, the man—a wiry figure with deep lines etched into his face—whirled on her, his thick Italian accent slicing through the air like a knife.

"Hey! Watch where you're going, huh? You blind or somethin'?"

His voice was sharp, laced with irritation, and his hands

flew up in exaggerated gestures, punctuating each word with frustration. His narrowed eyes bore into her, his expression twisted with condescension.

Clara's stomach clenched. Heat rushed to her cheeks as shame flooded her, making her feel unbearably small. "So… sorry," she stammered, her voice barely more than a whisper. But her apology didn't matter. The man was already muttering under his breath, his words thick with vulgarity and disdain.

"Stupid girl… no respect… people these days…"

She didn't wait to hear more. Her feet carried her away, faster and faster, her heart hammering against her ribs. She hated this feeling—the tightness in her chest, the way her mind spiraled into self-reproach. *Why wasn't I paying attention? Why do I always feel like I'm in the wrong?*

The man's words clung to her, heavy and unshakable, a cruel reminder of how easily the world could make her feel invisible—except, of course, when someone wanted to remind her just how insignificant she really was.

She tucked her hands into her coat pockets, her shoulders hunched as if to shield herself from the weight of the interaction. The city, once a place of wonder and possibility, now felt overwhelming and unwelcoming. Clara longed for the quiet comfort of her apartment, where she could retreat into her books and paintings and forget the noise of the outside world.

Clara has always known she's an introvert—someone who finds strength in solitude and thrives in quiet moments. She's hardworking and intelligent, qualities she takes pride in, even if they often go unnoticed in the bustling chaos of New York City. Despite the city's teeming population, making friends hasn't come easily. Instead, she finds comfort in observing the vibrant tapestry of life around her, losing herself in the rhythm of the city crowd.

When alone, Clara turns to books, her faithful companions

that offer escape and understanding. Over the years, she's grown weary of the noise—the endless political debates, the performative nature of social media, the constant barrage of opinions. It all feels overwhelming, disconnected from the simplicity and depth she craves. In her quiet world, Clara seeks authenticity, a refuge from the chaos, and a space where she can simply be herself.

A heavy sigh escaped Clara's lips as the suffocating weight of her own thoughts followed her down the grimy stairs. The subway station yawned open before her, a concrete throat exhaling a breath that was thick with the sweet, nauseating stench of decay—likely a dead rat festering in some unseen corner. It was a smell that mirrored the rot of her own anxieties, and she descended into the gloom, a solitary figure swallowed by the city's indifferent belly. The train rattled along the tracks, a blur of harsh fluorescent lights, muffled conversations, and the pungent mix of too many bodies crammed into too small a space. The motion was erratic, jerking forward, then slowing, then lurching again—but Clara barely noticed. She had found a quiet corner, folding herself into the seat, letting the chaos around her fade as her thoughts took over.

She replayed the senior manager's curt demand, the way his eyes skimmed over her like she was just another piece of office furniture. She thought about the men in their suits, the way they laughed easily, never once looking her way unless they needed something. And then there was Evelyn—the only person who ever seemed to truly *see* her. Her words still echoed in Clara's mind, a flicker of warmth against the cold doubt that had settled in her chest.

And then, there were her parents. Their belief in her. The sacrifices they had made. The nights she had spent hunched over textbooks, chasing a dream that once felt so certain. She wasn't just the mailroom girl. She was Clara—a woman who had worked too hard, sacrificed too much, to be reduced to an afterthought. She had a history. A passion for art. A fire inside her that no condescending glance or dismissive remark could extinguish.

Tears welled up in her eyes before she even realized they were coming. They spilled over, trailing down her cheeks like a quiet, unrelenting stream—grief, frustration, exhaustion, and maybe, just maybe, the smallest sliver of hope.

By the time the train screeched to a stop, her body felt leaden. She stepped onto the platform, the familiar path to her condo stretching before her, every step feeling heavier than the last. Her shoulders ached, her legs protested, but she kept moving, pushing through the weariness that clung to her like a second skin. Her pace was a reflex; a rhythm drummed into her by a lifetime of warnings. Especially at night, her footsteps would quicken from a walk to a near-jog, her keys already threaded between her knuckles like makeshift brass knuckles. It wasn't just the longing for the warm light of her own apartment that propelled her; it was a deep, primal urge for safety. The horrific stories she'd absorbed since girlhood—whispers of shadows that grabbed and alleys that swallowed women whole—echoed in every rustle of leaves and click of a distant heel. Every dark window was a watching eye, every silent man a potential threat. She didn't just walk fast; she fled the looming danger that every night held.

Finally, she reached her door. The key turned in the lock with a soft click, and the moment she stepped inside, a wave of exhaustion nearly took her to the floor. She kicked off her shoes, peeling away the weight of the day along with them, changed into her pajamas, and collapsed onto her bed.

The silence of her apartment wrapped around her like a heavy blanket, thick and unmoving. Only the faint hum of the refrigerator and the occasional whoosh of a car passing outside reminded her that the world hadn't stopped, even if she felt like she had. Lying on her bed, Clara stared up at the ceiling, her thoughts a tangled mess of frustration, doubt, and exhaustion.

Then, out of nowhere, a thought flickered to life—almost childish, but strangely comforting.

What if I had a superpower?

Not the kind in comic books—no capes, no laser vision, no bending the laws of physics. But something *useful*. Something that could've helped her *know*. Like the ability to see the future.

If she had known where this path would lead, would she have made different choices? Would she have stayed in Alberta, safe and familiar, instead of throwing herself into the chaos of New York? Or would she have still leaped—just with the reassurance that it would all be worth it in the end?

She exhaled softly, a small, tired smile tugging at the corners of her lips. Maybe knowing the future would take away the struggle, the uncertainty, the ache of wanting more but not knowing if she'd ever get it.

She imagined herself walking into the office tomorrow, knowing exactly how the day would unfold. She'd avoid the senior manager's last-minute demands, anticipate the printer jamming, and maybe even find a way to impress someone important. Maybe she'd see an opportunity before it happened—a chance to step out of the mailroom and into something bigger.

But then again, she thought, would knowing the future take away the thrill of the unknown? The small victories that came from figuring things out as she went? Clara sighed, her eyelids growing heavy. The idea of a superpower felt comforting, but it also reminded her that life, for all its frustrations, was still hers to shape.

As her thoughts drifted, Clara's breathing slowed, and the tension in her body began to melt away. The last thing she remembered before falling asleep was the faint glow of the city lights through her window, a quiet reminder that tomorrow is going to be another day in the history and hopefully something exciting is going to happen.

CHAPTER 2: SHINING NAILS

It was a bright, sunny Friday morning in late spring, and Clara woke up to the soft, golden glow of sunlight streaming through the blinds of her cozy little rental condo. She stretched lazily, savoring the warmth of the morning like a cat basking in a sunbeam. The sunlight danced across her bedroom, making her vibrant flower paintings in the corner come alive with color, as if they were blooming right before her eyes.

Fridays always had a special kind of magic for Clara. They were a sweet reward after a long workweek, a little reminder that the weekend was just around the corner. Sure, life could feel a bit routine at times, but Clara had a knack for finding joy in the little things. She tapped play on her favorite Mariah Carey playlist, letting the upbeat tunes fill her space through her adorable Bluetooth speaker. It was impossible not to smile as she hummed along, the music adding a sparkle to her morning.

While sorting packages and delivering mail in a downtown office building might not have been her dream job, Clara approached it with her signature optimism. It paid the bills, sure, but more than that, it gave her a chance to pursue her big dream in The Big Apple.

As Clara got ready for work, she hummed a little tune, transforming her dark curls into something resembling a masterpiece (or at least a Pinterest fail). She slipped into her trusty khaki pants and polo shirt—her "uniform of mystery and mail-sorting prowess"—and was about to grab her keys when "drama alert" erupted outside. Naturally, Clara couldn't resist. She stepped onto her tiny balcony, which was basically her front-row seat to the neighborhood's daily soap opera.

Down below, a woman's voice sliced through the morning air like a knife through butter. "Hey, do you even know how to drive? Or is this your way of proving the stereotype that men are terrible drivers?" Ouch. Clara leaned over the railing, popcorn-worthy entertainment unfolding before her eyes. A sleek red car had apparently decided to play chicken with a silver sedan at the intersection, and the sedan's driver—a woman in her mid-40s who clearly didn't have time for nonsense—was out of her car, hands on her hips, delivering a verbal smackdown that could've won her an Oscar for Best Sassy Comeback.

The guy in the red car looked like he'd just been told his Wi-Fi was being cut off—flustered, muttering something unintelligible, and peeling away like he'd just remembered he left the stove on. Clara couldn't help but smirk. Sure, the woman's words were sharper than a freshly sharpened pencil, but there was a certain "je ne sais quoi" in her tone that Clara couldn't help but admire. She wondered if this woman, like Clara, had endured her fair share of eye-roll-worthy gender jokes and was now serving up some well-deserved karma.

Clara gave a little nod of respect to the sassy queen below. "You go, girl," she muttered under her breath, before heading back inside, ready to tackle her day with a little extra sass of her own.

The memory slammed into Clara like an awkward flashback she hadn't signed up for. When she was 19 and just learning to drive, the older boy from next door—let's call him Mr. Unnecessary Commentary—had decided to grace her with his "hilarious" wisdom. "Watch out, everyone! Clara's behind the wheel. The stereotype about women drivers is about to come true!" he'd crowed, like he was auditioning for the role of World's Most Annoying Neighbor. At the time, Clara had forced a laugh, pretending it didn't bother her, but inside? Oh, inside she was cringing so hard she could've powered a small city with the sheer energy of her embarrassment.

She'd worked her tail off after that, practicing parallel parking until her steering wheel probably had permanent handprints and mastering defensive driving like her life depended on it (and honestly, it kind of did). But even now, over a decade later, the memory still popped up at the worst moments, like an uninvited guest at a party. It was the kind of thing that made her cheeks burn and her stomach twist, even though she knew she was a perfectly capable driver. Ugh, why did brains have to be so good at holding onto the most mortifying moments? Clara sighed, wishing she could just shove that memory into a mental shredder and be done with it.

Clara shook her head, pushing the thought aside as she grabbed her bag and headed out the door. The streets were bustling with the usual Friday morning rush, and Clara walked briskly, her mind still replaying the scene she saw from her balcony earlier. The woman's words had been rude, sure, but there was something empowering about her unapologetic tone. Clara wondered what it would be like to have that kind of confidence —to speak her mind without worrying about how others might perceive her.

Clara's morning commute was usually a blur—head down, lost in her thoughts, just trying to get through the chaos of the city. But today felt different. As she stepped into the subway, she couldn't help but notice how unusually clean and inviting it felt. It was as if the city had worked some overnight magic, and the results were downright refreshing. The floors sparkled, the walls looked freshly painted, and the air carried a subtle, comforting hint of citrus cleaner—like a cozy hug for her senses. It was the kind of small but meaningful change that made her pause and take it all in.

As she walked further, she spotted a group of men in snug work clothes scrubbing away at a stubborn patch of graffiti near a bench. Their dedication was evident, and Clara couldn't help but smile softly, feeling a quiet appreciation for their hard work. It was one of those little moments that reminded her of the good in people—even if their outfits were a bit… "fitted".

Just then, an elderly man nearly bumped into her but quickly stepped back, tipping his hat with a warm, apologetic smile. "Pardon me, miss," he said kindly, gesturing for her to go ahead. Clara felt a gentle warmth spread through her chest, like sipping a cup of tea on a chilly morning. "How lovely it would be if all men were as polite as this sweet gentleman," she thought, her heart lifting just a little. It was a small gesture, but it felt like a quiet reminder that kindness still existed in the world.

"It's okay," Clara smiled back. She watched as the man nodded shyly before disappearing into the crowd. She couldn't help but feel a little amused—and then she noticed something. The old man, along with many other men in the crowd, was wearing a neck band. Some were wide, almost covering the entire neck, while others were narrow, resting just above the Adam's apple. "Is this some new trend?" she wondered, intrigued.

As she stepped onto the subway, she found a seat nestled among a group of well-dressed women. Their elegant outfits and calm, composed energy added to the soothing atmosphere of the train. Clara settled into her seat, feeling a sense of comfort and belonging as the train hummed along, carrying her toward the day ahead. And then she noticed something that made her smile even wider—every single one of those women was wearing stylish yet practical shoes with flat heels. No sky-high stilettos, no pinched toes, just chic comfort. "Is this a new fashion trend?" she wondered, feeling a little spark of inspiration. Maybe, just maybe, the world was finally catching on, that women deserved both style and comfort.

As for the men's neck bands? Clara didn't know the reason behind them, but she thought they looked kind of cool.

Leaning back, Clara let the gentle rhythm of the train and the quiet solidarity of the women around her wrap her in a sense of calm. It was a morning that felt like a soft reminder: *Every day is a new day. You're moving forward. And there's beauty in the little things*. For the first time in a while, Clara felt a spark of morning excitement—for what the day might bring.

Before Clara arrived at the office building, she made a quick stop at the cozy coffee shop next door, a place she frequented for her morning treat. The aroma of freshly brewed coffee and warm pastries greeted her as she stepped inside, the chatter of customers blending with the soft hum of espresso machines. She ordered her usual: a creamy coffee with a generous dusting of cinnamon sugar on top and a crusty apple pie that always reminded her of autumn mornings as a child. As she waited in line, her mind wandered, but her attention was abruptly pulled to a conversation happening just a few feet away.

Two women, both impeccably dressed and exuding an air of confidence, were discussing a shocking news story from the previous night. Their voices were low but carried an edge of excitement. Clara couldn't help but eavesdrop.

"Did you hear about what happened last night?" one woman said, her eyes wide with a mix of disbelief and satisfaction. "A woman slammed a man after he tried to pickpocket her. They said he's in critical condition at the hospital. Can you believe it?"

Clara's heart skipped a beat. She froze, her grip tightening on her phone as she processed the words. A man in critical condition? Because of a woman? Her mind raced, and before she could stop herself, she blurted out, "What? Was that woman a professional MMA fighter or something?"

The moment the words left her mouth, the café seemed to go silent. All eyes turned to Clara. The woman who had initiated the discussion smirked, her glossy lips curling into a sly smile. "Aha, you're funny," she said, her tone dripping with savvy. "The man was lucky she only used one hand under level-6 anger on him.

But the doctors say he'll probably be in a wheelchair for the rest of his life."

Clara's jaw dropped. She felt a mix of shock, disbelief, and a strange sense of awe. Before she could respond, another woman chimed in, her voice sharp and unapologetic. "Yeah, I doubt he'll be pickpocketing anyone ever again. What an idiot."

"Men don't think straight sometimes," another added, rolling her eyes as she stirred her latte.

The room buzzed with a vibe so electric; it felt like a secret meeting of the coolest club in town. Clara stood there, half wondering if she'd accidentally walked into a scene from a movie. The women around her exchanged knowing glances and nods, as if they were all in on a joke the rest of the world hadn't caught onto yet. Clara couldn't help but glance around the café, her eyes catching details she'd somehow missed before. Every woman in the room had nails that could've been featured in a glossy magazine—some long and elegant, others short and practical, but all of them dazzling with intricate designs or bold, fearless colors. It was like a rainbow had exploded in the best possible way.

Their body language was a masterclass in confidence—relaxed but commanding, as if they didn't just occupy the space but "owned" it. Clara realized the coffee shop was packed, but not with the usual mix of frazzled commuters and laptop warriors. Today, it was a sanctuary of women—women with manicures that sparkled like tiny works of art, hairstyles so sleek they could've been carved from marble, and an air of confidence so unshakable it could've powered the city.

When they turned their gazes toward Clara, it wasn't intimidating—it was oddly comforting, like being wrapped in a warm, knowing hug. Their looks were a mix of amusement and curiosity, as if they were silently saying, "You're one of us, whether you know it yet or not." Clara felt a spark of amazement, like she'd stumbled into a hidden world where women ruled, nails were always on point, and confidence was the only dress code. It was comforting, empowering, and just a little bit magical.

Clara's heart raced as she grabbed her coffee and pie, the barista sliding them across the counter with a smile that felt way too knowing for 8 a.m. She mumbled a hurried "thanks" and bolted out of the café like she always did on chaotic mornings, but this time, her mind was spinning. The conversation she'd just overheard—or maybe been *part of*?—clung to her thoughts like static, refusing to let go.

As she stepped onto the busy streets of Manhattan, her head was already swimming, but then she noticed it. Everywhere she looked, it was there. The same thing. The *phenomenon*. It was like the universe had decided to play a prank on her, and she was the only one who hadn't gotten the memo.

She couldn't help but noticing women dominated the sidewalks, walking with their heads held high, their outfits sharp and purposeful. Their nails glinted in the sunlight, catching Clara's eye at every turn. Some were painted with intricate patterns—floral designs, geometric shapes, even tiny works of art. Others sparkled with metallic finishes or bold, solid colors. It was as if every woman had taken extra care to present herself with confidence and flair.

Clara's gaze darted from one woman to another, her mind racing. She noticed how men seemed to step aside as women passed, often apologizing even when they weren't at fault. It was a subtle shift, but it was there—a quiet acknowledgment of the power these women carried. And again, most men were wearing a neck band. Some bands are very colorful, and some are just black or white. Clara felt a strange mix of emotions: confusion, curiosity, and a growing sense of empowerment she hadn't expected.

Her chest tightened, her thoughts jumbled, and for a moment, she felt like she was stuck in some bizarre dream where nothing made sense but everyone else acted like it was totally normal. Overwhelmed and utterly confused, Clara clutched her coffee tighter, wondering if she'd accidentally stepped into a parallel universe on her way to work.

Clara reached for her phone, desperate to check the news for any updates, but the screen remained stubbornly black. "No, no, no," she muttered under her breath, pressing the power button repeatedly. The battery was completely dead. Frustration bubbled up inside her as she shoved the useless device back into her pocket. As she lifted her gaze, Clara noticed a group of men nearby, their expressions etched with unease. They averted their eyes, deliberately avoiding any contact with her, and swiftly moved away, creating an invisible but palpable distance. The air grew heavy with unspoken tension, their hurried retreat leaving her feeling both exposed and isolated. Rather confused and embarrassed, she quickened her pace, practically speed-walking toward the office, her mind racing with unanswered questions. The work computer was her only hope now—she had to find some answers, anything to make sense of the strangeness swirling around her.

As she approached the office building, Clara couldn't shake the feeling that something had changed—not just in the world around her, but within herself. The shock of the morning's events lingered, but so did a newfound determination. She didn't know what it all meant yet, but she was ready to find out.

CHAPTER 3: FIREN

Walking into the office building, Clara felt the same palpable shift in energy that she had noticed outside. The air seemed charged, almost electric, as if the building itself had absorbed the new dynamic. Women moved through the lobby with purpose, their shoes without high heels taping loudly against the marble floor, their voices carrying a confident authority. Men, on the other hand, with their neck bands and tight suits, seemed to tread more carefully, their movements subdued, their voices quieter, as if they were acutely aware of the invisible lines they shouldn't cross. Clara's pulse quickened as she took it all in, the atmosphere thick with an unspoken tension that made her skin prickle.

She hurried to her desk, her mind racing with questions. Dropping her bag and coffee onto the surface, she immediately opened her workstation, her fingers trembling slightly as she typed. She needed to know more about what she had overheard at the café. Her heart pounded in her chest as she searched for news about the incident from last night. The screen filled with headlines, each more shocking than the last:

"Woman's Self-Defense Leaves Pickpocket in Critical Condition."

"Another case of Severe Nerve Damage on reckless theft man."

"Doctors Warn of Permanent Paralysis After Attack."

Clara's breath hitched as she clicked on the first article. The details were graphic and unsettling. The man, identified as a known pickpocket, had approached the woman in a crowded subway station. When he attempted to steal her wallet, she reacted with what witnesses described as "lightning-fast precision." According to the report, she had slammed him with such force that he collapsed instantly, his body convulsing as if struck by an invisible force. Paramedics rushed him to the hospital, where doctors discovered severe nerve damage in his head and neck area. The article mentioned something called "Firen," a term Clara had never heard before.

Her stomach churned as she read on. The woman at the café had mentioned "level-6 anger," and now Clara understood why. The article explained that Firen was a chemical released from women's nails when they experienced intense anger. It was a defense mechanism, triggered by environmental stressors, and its effects were devastating. If a man came within two inches of a woman's nails during this release, the chemical could penetrate his skin, targeting his nervous system. The severity of the damage depended on the level of anger, categorized from 1 to 10.

Clara's hands shook as she scrolled further. At level 1, Firen caused mild muscle cramps—a warning, perhaps, to back off. But at level 6, like in the case of the pickpocket, the dosage was high enough to cause severe nerve damage, potentially leading to lifelong paralysis. The article included a diagram showing how the chemical traveled through the body, attacking the brain and spinal cord. Clara's chest tightened as she imagined the man in the hospital, his body broken, his future uncertain.

She couldn't stop herself from digging deeper. She searched for "Firen" and found a flood of information. Scientific studies, news reports, and even government advisories warned men to maintain a safe distance from women in moments of heightened tension. There were charts detailing the levels of anger and their corresponding effects:

Level 1-3: Mild to moderate reactions—muscle cramps,

temporary numbness.

Level 4-6: Severe nerve damage, potential paralysis.

Level 7-9: Brain damage, risk of coma.

Level 10: Vegetative state or death.

Clara's mind reeled. She stared at her own nails, short and unpolished, and wondered how something so small could wield such power. The thought was both terrifying and awe-inspiring. She recalled the women at the café, their shining nails and unshakable confidence. Now it all made sense. They weren't just stylish—they were armed, in a way Clara had never imagined.

As she sat there, the office buzzed around her, but Clara felt like she was in a bubble, the weight of what she had learned pressing down on her. She glanced at her female coworkers, their nails glinting under the fluorescent lights. One woman tapped her pen against her desk, her long, manicured nails clicking rhythmically. Another leaned back in her chair, her fingers steepled, her nails painted a deep, metallic red. Clara's heart raced as she realized the power they carried—literally at their fingertips.

Her mind spinning as she tried to make sense of everything. She looked at the date on her screen. It was surprisingly correct and intact. How had the world shifted so drastically overnight? It felt like she had woken up in a parallel universe, one where women were the physically dominant gender, and men walked on eggshells, their confidence replaced by caution. She pinched herself hard, then slapped her cheek for good measure. The sharp sting made her wince. "Okay, not a dream," she muttered under her breath, her voice trembling. "What kind of Earth am I on?"

Despite of the confusion and stress, she doesn't feel her life is in danger so far in this new environment. She took a deep breath, steadying herself, and turned back to her work computer.

Her natural talent for studying history quickly came to the forefront, guiding her as she began to methodically research and analyze the information before her. Her fingers flew across the keyboard as she dove deeper into the history of humanity, desperate for answers. What she found left her breathless. For thousands of years, human history had been male-dominated—wars, empires, and societies built on the backs of men's physical strength and political power. But then, six decades ago, something extraordinary happened. A shift in the sun's magnetic field triggered a series of mutations in the female body. Scientists called it the "Solar Reversal," a cosmic event that rewired women's biology in ways no one could have predicted.

Clara's eyes widened as she read about the changes. Starting from puberty and throughout the rest of life, women's bodies developed a new neural network, one that connected directly to their nails. This network allowed them to release a potent chemical called "Firen", a defense mechanism triggered by anger or stress. The chemical was deadly to men, capable of causing anything from mild discomfort to severe nerve damage, paralysis, or even death, depending on the level of anger. The article included diagrams of the neural pathways, showing how the chemical traveled from the brain to the fingertips, ready to be unleashed at a moment's notice.

As Clara's research deepened, she found out that in the wake of the Solar Reversal six decades ago in 1953, the world underwent a seismic shift as women's newfound physical dominance rewrote the fabric of society. The first decade saw the collapse of traditional power structures. Male-dominated industries, from politics to sports, crumbled as women, armed with the lethal potential of Firen, demanded right in every social aspects—and got it, sadly with massive casualty on males globally. Governments scrambled to adapt, passing laws to protect men from accidental or intentional harm, while women ascended to leadership roles at an unprecedented rate.

By the 1960s, education systems had transformed. Schools

emphasized emotional regulation and conflict resolution for women, while men were taught to navigate a world where physical strength no longer guaranteed dominance. The workplace evolved, too, with women dominating fields like law enforcement, military, and engineering, while men gravitated toward roles in caregiving and creative industries. The 1970s brought cultural upheaval. Art, literature, and media shifted to reflect the new reality, celebrating female strength and resilience. Men, once the default protagonists, became supporting characters in narratives that centered on women's experiences. Relationships also changed, with traditional gender roles dissolving in favor of partnerships built on mutual respect and emotional connection. By today, the world had stabilized into a new equilibrium. Women's dominance was no longer questioned, and men had adapted to their altered roles.

Clara stared at her own hands, her short, unpolished nails suddenly feeling like weapons she didn't know how to wield. Her heart raced as she imagined the power coursing through every woman around her. It was both terrifying and awe-inspiring. She felt a pang of sympathy for the men outside, their once-unquestioned dominance now reduced to wary glances and careful movements.

She looked at the date on her computer: June 6th, 2025. Exactly what she thought it would be when she woke up this morning.

Just then, a loud crash shattered the silence. Clara jumped in her seat, her heart leaping into her throat. The sound came from the meeting room, followed by Evelyn's sharp voice. "Jesus Christ! Quit being so clumsy! You're lucky I kept my hands away from you. It could've ended really bad."

Clara's stomach churned as she recognized the tone—a mix of frustration and barely restrained anger. She heard a man's voice next, shaky and apologetic. "I'm so sorry. Thank you for being considerate. I'll be more careful next time."

"Good," Evelyn said with an eye roll so dramatic it could've won an award, "I don't have time to deal with another lawsuit on office abuse. Some of us actually have important work to do."

Clara found Evelyn's words oddly arrogant and aggressive, and so unlike her. But Clara's curiosity got the better of her. She stood up and peeked out of her desk, her eyes widening at the scene in the meeting room. It's Evelyn, who stood at the head of the table, her arms crossed and her nails—long, sharp, and painted a fiery red—tapping impatiently against her elbow. A middle-aged man stood in front of her, his shoulders hunched, his face pale as he nodded along to her reprimand. Around them, a dozen staff members watched silently, most of them women. Their expressions ranged from mild amusement to outright indifference, as if this were just another day in the office.

Clara's chest tightened as she took in the dynamics. The man looked utterly defeated, his confidence stripped away by Evelyn's words and the unspoken threat of Firen. The women in the room, on the other hand, exuded a quiet authority, their polished nails glinting under the fluorescent lights like tiny weapons. Clara couldn't help but feel a mix of emotions—empathy for the man, awe at Evelyn's dominance, and a growing unease about her own place in this new world.

She slipped back into her seat, her mind racing. The office felt different now, the air thick with tension and unspoken power dynamics. Clara glanced at her coworkers, their nails gleaming as they typed or sipped coffee, and wondered how long it would take for her to adjust to this reality. The world had changed overnight, and she was only just beginning to understand the implications.

As she sat there, her thoughts swirling, one thing became painfully clear: this wasn't just a shift in power—it was a complete upheaval of everything she thought she knew. And Clara had no idea where she fit into it all.

CHAPTER 4: EASY DAY OF WORK

After two hours of intense research on Firen, Clara finally leaned back in her chair, her mind buzzing with information. She glanced at the clock and gasped—it was already 10:30 a.m. Normally, she'd be buried under a mountain of packages and envelopes in the mailroom by now, but today felt different. The office was unusually quiet, almost serene, except for the faint echo of Evelyn's voice still lecturing someone in the meeting room.

Clara had a quick idea to check her bank balance in this new world. Her fingers hovered over the keyboard as she typed in the familiar password - the same one she'd used for years - a combination of her childhood dog's name and the year she'd gotten her first real paycheck. When the banking dashboard loaded, she let out a wry chuckle that held no real amusement. There it was, staring back at her in unforgiving digits: **$368.27**. Exactly the same paltry sum as before.

"Well, universe," she muttered to the empty room, "guess I'll be keeping my day job after all." Clara sighed, stretching her arms, and her eyes landed on the schedule panel she had pinned to the wall weeks ago.

Her breath caught in her throat. The panel still bore her handwriting, but the times had changed. Instead of "Mailroom opens at 8:30 a.m.," it now read, "Mailroom opens at 10:30 a.m." And where it once said, "Delivery time: 4 p.m.," it now declared,

"All deliveries completed by 1 p.m." Below that, in bold letters, was the most shocking change of all: "Workday ends at 2 p.m."

Clara's heart leapt with a mix of disbelief and joy. "What kind of gracious work hours are these?" she whispered to herself, a smile spreading across her face. She couldn't help but chuckle. "I guess this is the sweet work/life balance under female leadership," she thought, feeling a wave of gratitude wash over her. For the first time in years, her job didn't feel like a grind. It felt... manageable. Even enjoyable.

Just as she was basking in the glow of this revelation, a hesitant voice broke her reverie. "Ms. Clara, how's your morning so far?" She looked up and blinked in surprise. It was the same guy who had stormed into the mailroom yesterday, dropping off a package at the last minute and demanding it be sent out "ASAP" in a tone that had made her blood boil. But today, he was a different person. His shoulders were slightly hunched, his eyes soft and almost shy. In his hands, he held a neatly wrapped box, which he presented to her with a tentative smile.

"Could you please help me send this to the Los Angeles office?" he asked, his voice gentle and pleading. "The boss needs it by Monday morning. I'm... I'm on my last straw here. It's been a really rough week."

Clara stared at him, momentarily speechless. She wasn't used to this version of him—the one who spoke with humility instead of entitlement. Her mind raced, trying to reconcile the man in front of her with the one from yesterday. Before she could respond, he added, "I totally understand it's short notice. I'll get you a nice lunch if you can help me out. Please."

His tone was so earnest, so unlike the condescending attitude she'd come to expect, that Clara felt her resistance melt away. A small smile tugged at her lips. "Okay," she said, her voice warm but firm. "I'll see what I can do." She took the package and set it aside, already mentally rearranging her schedule to accommodate the request.

"Thank you. Thank you. Thank you. You're the best," he gushed, his relief palpable. "What would you like for lunch? Tuna? Or wings?"

Clara couldn't help but chuckle softly. "Wings are fine," she replied, amused by his eagerness. As he turned to leave, she called after him, "Wait, what's your name again?"

He spun around, his face lighting up with a genuine smile. "My apologies. I'm Bob. It's so great to work with you."

Clara instinctively started to extend her hand for a handshake, but Bob's eyes flicked to her fingers, and he froze. For a split second, his expression shifted to one of unease, and Clara suddenly remembered why men no longer shook hands in this world. She withdrew her hand quickly, her cheeks flushing with embarrassment. "Right," she said, forcing a smile. "Nice to meet you, Bob."

As he walked away, Clara sat back in her chair, her emotions swirling. The morning had been a rollercoaster—shock, joy, confusion, and now a strange sense of empowerment. She glanced at the package on her desk, then at the revised schedule on the wall, and let out a slow breath. The world had changed, and so had she. And for the first time in a long time, Clara felt like she was exactly where she was meant to be.

The morning rolled on, and soon a few more colleagues trickled into the mailroom to drop off their packages. Most of them were male assistants to department heads, and Clara couldn't help but notice how polite and dedicated they all seemed. Each one greeted her with a smile, some even offering small compliments about how organized the mailroom looked. Clara found herself enjoying the interactions, the time slipping by faster than she expected. By 1 p.m., the room was buzzing with a calm, productive energy.

Right on schedule, the delivery guy arrived. He was big and tall, with broad shoulders and a friendly face. Despite his imposing physique, he was soft-spoken, his voice warm and gentle as he greeted Clara. "Afternoon," he said with a smile, his eyes crinkling at the corners. "Ready to get these out?"

Clara nodded, guiding him to the stack of neatly packed boxes. As he began lifting the heavy loads with ease, Clara absentmindedly reached out to steady one of the boxes. The moment her hand brushed against it, the delivery guy froze, his eyes darting to her fingers with a flicker of unease. Clara quickly pulled her hand back, offering an apologetic smile. "Sorry about that," she said, her tone light. He chuckled nervously; his cheeks tinged with pink. "No worries," he replied, though his movements became even more careful as he finished loading the packages.

After he left, Clara tidied up her desk, feeling a sense of accomplishment. Just as she was about to pack up for the day, Bob appeared in the doorway, holding a lunch box. "I got your wings," he said, his voice cheerful but slightly shy. "Thanks for your efforts today."

Clara couldn't help but laugh. "No problem," she replied, taking the box from him. The smell of crispy, seasoned wings wafted through the air, making her stomach growl in anticipation. Bob lingered for a moment, looking like he wanted to say more, but before he could, Evelyn strolled in, her nails shine like diamonds confidently as she waived hi.

"What's up, girl?" Evelyn said, her tone playful as she leaned against the doorframe. She glanced at Bob, then back at Clara, a mischievous grin spreading across her face. "I see you've hooked up with the bubbly Bob."

Bob's cheeks turned bright red, and he stammered something unintelligible before quickly excusing himself. Clara laughed, shaking her head as she watched him retreat. Evelyn's teasing was lighthearted, and Clara realized that in this world, the dynamics between women and men had shifted in a way that felt almost… refreshing. It wasn't uncommon for women to tease the men in the office, a playful reversal of how things used to be. And Evelyn, with her sharp wit and confident demeanor, was clearly enjoying it.

Clara couldn't keep it to herself any longer. The whirlwind of the last 24 hours had left her buzzing with questions, and she needed someone to confide in. Evelyn, with her sharp wit and no-nonsense attitude, seemed like the perfect person. Clara approached her cautiously, a mischievous glint in her eye. "Hey, Evelyn," she began, lowering her voice to a conspiratorial whisper. "This might sound… unusual, but can we talk in private? I've got something crazy—and honestly, kind of exciting—to tell you."

Evelyn's eyebrows shot up, and a sly grin spread across her face. "Woo, I like the sound of that," she said, her tone dripping with intrigue. "Come to my office. Now."

Clara blinked, caught off guard. "Wait… you have an office?" she asked, her surprise evident. The last she remembered, Evelyn was a project manager crammed into one of the small cubicles, surrounded by male colleagues who seemed to dominate the space. But as they walked through the office aisles, Clara's eyes widened. The entire building had transformed.

Gone were the sterile, uninspired hallways. In their place were beautifully decorated flower arrangements, their vibrant colors and fresh scents filling the air. Large, luxurious nursing rooms for working moms dotted the floor, their doors adorned with cheerful artwork. The most striking change, however, was the office layout itself. The largest, most independent offices now belonged to female department heads, their names etched on sleek plaques. The gender ratio had flipped entirely—women dominated the space, their confidence and authority prevailing.

As they passed a group of male colleagues among those small cubes, Clara noticed how diligently they worked, their demeanor humble and focused. No chitchat but bearing their heads down on piles of files. It was a stark contrast to the way things used to be, and Clara couldn't help but feel a thrill of curiosity about how this new world operated.

When they finally reached Evelyn's office, Clara's jaw nearly hit the floor. It wasn't just any office—it was a corner suite, complete with floor-to-ceiling windows, a plush leather chair, and a desk that looked like it belonged to a CEO. Clara stopped in shock when she saw the title on the office door. "Evelyn… you're the director manager now?" Clara asked, her voice tinged with awe.

Evelyn smirked, leaning back in her chair with the ease of someone who knew exactly how much power she held. "Oh, honey," she said, her tone playful yet commanding. "You've got a lot to catch up on, don't you? Now, sit down and spill. What's this 'crazy but exciting' thing you've been dying to tell me?"

Clara sat, her mind racing with possibilities. She had no idea where this conversation would lead, but one thing was certain: Evelyn was about to make things even more interesting.

CHAPTER 5: BEEKWOMEN HOTEL

Clara's mind was a whirlwind of confusion and excitement; her thoughts tangled like a ball of yarn she couldn't quite unravel. She shifted uncomfortably, her fingers fidgeting with the hem of her blouse as she glanced around Evelyn's impeccably designed office. The plush white leather couch, the sleek red wood buffet table adorned with bottles of Fiji water—it all felt both familiar and alien at the same time. Her throat was dry, her stomach empty, and the sight of the water made her realize she hadn't eaten or drunk anything all day. Her hands trembled slightly as she reached for a bottle, her voice barely above a whisper.

"Can I have some water?" Clara asked, her words stumbling out in a rush.

Evelyn, seated across from her, leaned back in her chair with an air of calm authority. Her piercing deep blue eyes locked onto Clara's stressed face, studying her with a mix of curiosity and amusement. "Sure," Evelyn replied, her tone smooth and unhurried. She watched as Clara practically lunged for the bottle, gulping down the water like she'd been stranded in a desert. A small, intrigued smile played on Evelyn's lips. "I'm in no rush. Whenever you're ready."

Clara set the bottle down with a soft clink, wiping the droplets from her chin with the back of her hand. She took a deep breath, her chest rising and falling as she gathered her courage. Her eyes met Evelyn's again, and for a moment, she felt like those blue eyes could see straight through her. "This may sound insane," Clara began, her voice shaky but determined, "but I think I'm from a different parallel universe. A place where things are… very different from here. Except, oddly enough, we still work in the same building, the same company, and—surprisingly—we're on good terms." She paused, her hands gesturing wildly as she tried to piece together her thoughts. "But since I woke up this morning, everything's changed. Women are dominating society here because of…Firen? And I was…I was from a world where men ruled, just yesterday."

As Clara rambled, her words tumbling out in a frantic jumble, she braced herself for ridicule or disbelief. But Evelyn didn't laugh. She didn't even blink. Instead, she leaned forward slightly, her smile widening into something warm and knowing. "Welcome to the era of Roses," Evelyn said calmly, her voice like a soothing balm.

Clara's brows furrowed in confusion, her mouth opening and closing as she struggled to find the right response. "You…you know?" she finally managed to stammer.

Evelyn's smile turned almost mischievous. "Yes, I know. You're not the first one to come to me with this."

Clara's eyes widened, a spark of hope and excitement flickering in her chest. "You're saying there are more people like me? People who've…jumped into this world?" Her voice rose with each word, her hands gripping the edge of the couch as if to anchor herself. "I hope they're all women. I don't think the men from my universe would appreciate this place very much."

Evelyn let out a rich, hearty laugh, the sound filling the room. "Now, that's the spirit!" she exclaimed, her eyes sparkling with delight. She gestured toward the window, where the city skyline glittered in the afternoon sun. "The ladies here usually finish work around 2 p.m. If you're interested, you should join us for a drink. We have a private room at the Beekwomen Hotel."

Clara blinked, her mind catching on the name. "You mean

the Beekmen Hotel? Oh…wait. I see. It's Beekwomen now." A delighted grin spread across her face, the absurdity of it all finally sinking in.

Evelyn chuckled, reaching for a sleek business card on her desk. She slid it across the table toward Clara. "Here," she said, her tone warm and inviting. "Call this number when you get to the hotel. Tell the person on the phone that you're my guest for today. They'll show you to the room." She leaned back again, her smile softening. "I'm sure all the other ladies will be thrilled to meet you."

Clara's heart raced, a mix of relief, excitement, and curiosity brewing inside her. She picked up the card, her fingers tracing the elegant embossed letters. For the first time since she'd woken up in this strange new world, she felt a glimmer of understanding—and the thrill of something extraordinary about to unfold.

"Oh, okay! I guess I'll see you there, then!" Clara exclaimed, her voice bubbling with excitement. She clutched the paper tightly in her hands, as if they were a golden ticket to something extraordinary. A wide, almost giddy smile spread across her face, her eyes sparkling with anticipation.

Evelyn gave a subtle nod, her lips curving into a warm yet composed smile. "See you soon," she said, her voice smooth and steady, the kind of tone that comes from someone who's seen it all and isn't easily rattled. Her gaze lingered on Clara for a moment, like a mentor watching a protégé step into their power. There was a quiet confidence in her expression, as if she already knew Clara was about to embark on something extraordinary.

Clara had just stepped one foot out of Evelyn's office when she turned back, curiosity getting the better of her. "Oh, one more thing—what's with the bands all the men are wearing around their necks? Is that some kind of male fashion trend here?"

"Ah, that." Evelyn's lips twitched into a knowing smirk. "They're to cover their Adam's apples. It's like how women used to feel pressured to wear bras—just another part of the male body-shaming machine in this world. Funny, isn't it? Meanwhile, in the summer, you'll see women strolling down the street braless or lounging topless on the beach. Oh, and if you really want a laugh, look up 'mani suits.' They're basically the male version of bikinis these days." Her smirk deepened, as if she were sharing a delicious secret.

Clara stood frozen for a moment, processing the revelation. "Huh… interesting," she finally said, a slow smirk spreading across her own face. "Thanks for that." With a shake of her head and a chuckle, she stepped out of the office. "See you later," she called over her shoulder, her mind buzzing with the absurdity of it all.

As she walked away, Clara couldn't help but feel a mix of amusement and vindication. The world was changing, all right—just not in the ways anyone expected. And somehow, that made her feel a little more hopeful about the future.

The clock struck 2 PM, and like clockwork, Clara joined the stream of women flooding out of the office, their laughter and relaxed chatter filling the elevator. But as she glanced back, she noticed something odd—nearly all the men were still hunched over their desks, typing furiously. "Huh. I guess men have to work harder in this world", she mused, tucking her hands into the deep pockets of her practical yet stylish trousers.

Stepping onto the sunlit streets of Manhattan, Clara was immediately struck by the scene around her. The storefronts that once flaunted women's luxury handbags and skincare now gleamed with displays of men's cosmetics, form-fitting suits, and an array of wigs in every shade imaginable. Crowds of men flitted in and out, browsing silk scarves and debating the merits of different contouring palettes.

She couldn't help but smirk at the fashion dichotomy. Women strode by in sleek, functional clothing—roomy blazers, trousers with 'actual pockets', and comfortable loafers—while men teetered in snug, vibrantly colored ensembles, their tiny pockets clearly useless given the oversized designer totes swinging from their arms. "Some things never change", she thought wryly. "Just... reversed."

Then, a voice—smooth as honey and dripping with charm—caught her attention. A massive digital billboard outside a high-end menswear boutique flashed to life, showcasing a breathtakingly handsome young man lounging against a desk. His ice-blue eyes sparkled like gemstones, his pearl necklace glinting against a deep V-neck shirt that left little to the imagination. His golden tan looked airbrushed to perfection, and his legs, crossed at the ankle, were hairless and gleaming beneath a scandalously tight yellow skirt that hugged every curve.

"Renaissance for Respect in High Standard," the ad purred.

Clara blinked. The image was... "a lot". Not just because she wasn't used to seeing men displayed like that, but because—she realized with a jolt—it wasn't so different from the way women had been marketed to in "her" world. The discomfort settled in her chest. Had she ever questioned those ads back home? Or had she just accepted them as normal?

Shaking off the thought, she continued down the street, weaving through the crowds of Times Square. The towering screens, once dominated by female celebrities and lingerie models, now featured an endless parade of male faces—flawlessly contoured, eyebrows meticulously groomed, lashes darkened with mascara. Every man she passed seemed meticulously polished, their skin dewy, their hair styled to perfection. Yet none wore the bold, glittering nail art that adorned the hands of the women around them—women who walked with an easy confidence, their postures relaxed, their laughter loud and unapologetic.

At a crosswalk, Clara paused beside a group of parents waiting with strollers. A few men cooed over their babies, adjusting their designer diaper bags while their wives (or girlfriends?), or checked their bags impatiently. "At least men are still getting wives and having children", Clara thought, biting back a smirk. The sarcasm tasted strange on her tongue.

But what surprised her most wasn't the fashion, the ads, or even the gender dynamics. It was how quickly she'd adapted. Already, the female-dominated energy of this world felt… "normal". And "that" realization unsettled her more than anything else.

What else, she wondered, would this world reveal to her? And more importantly—what would it force her to question about her own?

2 HOURS LATER:

Clara stepped into the grand lobby of the Beekwomen Hotel, her heart pounding like a drum, a whirlwind of excitement and nervousness surging through her veins. The sheer opulence of the place was staggering—crystal chandeliers hung like constellations above, their light cascading onto gleaming marble floors, while the air carried the intoxicating scent of jasmine and unapologetic luxury. She clutched the business card Evelyn had given her, her fingers trembling with anticipation as she approached the concierge. After a brief exchange, she was whisked away to a private room on the top floor, where the city skyline stretched out before her like a glittering sea of possibilities.

As the door swung open, Clara's breath caught in her throat. The scene before her was nothing short of breathtaking. Five women sat around a sleek, modern table, each radiating an aura of power and confidence that seemed to electrify the room. They turned to her with warm, welcoming smiles, and Evelyn rose to greet her. "Clara, come in!" she said, her voice brimming with enthusiasm. "Let me introduce you to some truly extraordinary women."

First was Sarah, the head of the NYPD. Her uniform was immaculate, her posture commanding, and her handshake firm.

"Welcome, Clara! Sarah Marshall. You can call me Sarah," she said with a grin that could light up the darkest alley. "I know this world might feel like a shock, but trust me, it's the 'good' kind of shock."

Clara's eyes darted to Sarah's badge. "Are you NYPD?" she asked, her voice tinged with awe.

"Darling, yes. I'm the 'commissioner' of the NYPD," Sarah replied, her tone dripping with pride. "Back in my old world, I was constantly fighting to prove myself in a male-dominated field. Here, I didn't have to fight any man—just work alongside incredible sisters. Now, I run the largest police force in the country, with 99% of officers being women. And let me tell you, it's been the most fulfilling experience of my life."

Clara's jaw dropped. "Wait, are you saying the majority of police officers are women now?"

Sarah chuckled. "Oh, absolutely. With the physical advantages women have through deadly Firen, it's no surprise. But it's not just about strength—it's about strategy, empathy, and leadership. And we're 'killing' it."

Next to Sarah was Emily Jones, the Navy Admiral, her sharp gaze cutting through the room like a blade. She leaned back in her chair, her medals glinting like stars. "Firen didn't just level the playing field—it catapulted women into dominance in every profession," she said, her voice steady and commanding. "But let's be honest, women were always gifted in handling conflict and high-stress situations. Even before the era of Roses, we had the strategic thinking and empathetic communication skills to outshine men. But back in my old world, our voices were often drowned out by male leadership. In some places, women couldn't even make decisions about their own bodies. Here, I'm leading an entire fleet. And the best part? No one questions my decisions because of my gender. I'm judged purely on my skills and leadership. It's liberating."

Clara's eyes widened. "Are soldiers mainly women now too?"

Emily smirked. "Oh, we still hire men for technical roles. Some of them are excellent technicians, and we have male soldiers who focus on, well, 'entertaining' the crew. Life on a ship can get monotonous, and our boys are quite the performers. You should see our annual Navy Christmas party—it's a spectacle."

"Emily, don't scare her with your department of boy escorts just yet," interjected by Linda, the president of a media conglomerate, her voice dripping with playful sarcasm. "Welcome, Clara. I'm Linda Fredman, founder of LindAI Media. Welcome to the era of Roses."

"The era of Roses?" Clara repeated, her curiosity piqued. "Is that what it's officially called now?"

"You bet," Linda, around the same age as Clara, said with a sly smile. "Thanks to my AI media feed, the term caught on about two years ago. Media shapes how we see the world, and here, we're telling stories that empower women and dismantle male aggression. In my old life, I was stuck producing content that catered to male fantasies. I worked my ass off, barely scraping by, while my old boss sat in his chamber making sexist jokes with his buddies. Here, I'm changing the narrative. It's not just a job—it's a 'mission'."

Nancy Alvarez, the president of a major health insurance company, chimed in next. Her warm, approachable energy was a stark contrast to the weight of her words. "In my old world, I was constantly overlooked for promotions, even though I was more qualified than my male colleagues. Here, I've built a company that's revolutionizing healthcare access for women and marginalized communities. The support system in this society is unparalleled—women lift each other up instead of tearing each other down."

"And let's not forget the postpartum debt your company helped design," Linda added with a wink. "I hear the Europeans are adopting it now too."

Nancy nodded. "It's not a bad idea. It's reduced the physical and mental stress on women significantly. Insurance claims have dropped, and women are thriving."

Sarah rolled her eyes. "Yeah, but let's not ignore the spike in male suicides. Four out of five men suffer from postpartum depression because of the debt burden on top of household duties. It's a double-edged sword."

Clara's brow furrowed. "Wait, what's postpartum debt?"

Sarah sighed. "It's a maximum $150,000 loan given to house husbands for three years of postpartum care. It was designed to support full-time dads, but some men can't handle the stress. They turn to drugs, gambling, or worse. It's a tragic side effect of this new world."

Nancy nodded solemnly. "We're working on mental health support for these men, but many are too ashamed to seek help. They're obsessed with maintaining the perfect husband image, and it's destroying them."

Linda sighed. "It's the inevitable insecurity this world has given men. We're doing our best to balance it, but until artificial sperms are perfected, we'll need men to stick around."

"Yeah"; "Of course"; "It may come sooner than you think"; "I don't know. I liked the boys in my penthouse."; "You never know what mutation might come out next time between men and women. We might as well just enjoy our time for now!"; "Do you want to see this boy I hooked up last weekend?"; "Nice butt. He looks very cute. 21? 22? Good for you!" women in the room continued to discuss their opinions on men.

Clara shifted slightly in her plush chair, her fingers tightening around the stem of her wine glass as the conversation took a turn that made her stomach twist. The women around the table—powerful, confident, and unapologetic—had begun to trade lighthearted, almost dismissive comments about men. They joked about their perceived inadequacies, their struggles to adapt to this new world, and their roles as secondary players in a society now shaped by women. Each remark was met with laughter, a ripple of amusement that filled the room, but Clara felt a pang of discomfort settle in her chest.

She glanced around the table, her smile faltering for just a moment. These women were extraordinary—leaders, visionaries, trailblazers—and she admired them deeply. Yet, the casual way they spoke about men, as though they were relics of a bygone era, left her uneasy. It wasn't that she disagreed with the shift in power; after all, she had already begun to embrace the freedoms and opportunities this new world offered. But there was something about the tone, the almost gleeful dismissal, that felt… off. It reminded her of the way men had once spoken about women in her old world—reductive, condescending, and dismissive.

Clara's mind raced as she weighed her options. Should she speak up? Should she voice her discomfort and risk being seen as ungrateful or out of touch? This was her first high-end private meeting in this new world, a world she was still learning to navigate. She didn't want to be the buzzkill, the one who disrupted the flow of camaraderie and confidence that filled the room. These women had welcomed her, supported her, and offered her a chance to rebuild her life. The last thing she wanted was to alienate them.

So, she forced a smile, nodding along as the conversation continued. She laughed when it seemed appropriate, though the sound felt hollow in her ears. Inside, a quiet storm brewed—a mix of guilt, confusion, and a growing sense of moral unease. She told herself it was just banter, harmless jokes among friends. But deep down, she couldn't shake the feeling that something about it wasn't right.

As the night goes on, Clara found herself retreating slightly, her contributions to the conversation growing quieter, more reserved. She listened intently, her mind wrestling with the conflict within her. She thought to herself, 'all these women were from her old world before they landed in this new society. They mindset had switched significantly.'

When Clara stood to get more drinks, her emotions a tangled knot in her chest. Evelyn caught her arm as she turned to the bottles, her expression softening with concern. "Clara, are you alright? You seemed a little quiet."

Clara hesitated, her heart pounding. For a moment, she considered brushing it off, offering a polite excuse about being tired or overwhelmed. But something in Evelyn's gaze—warm, understanding, and genuinely caring—made her pause. "I… I guess I just felt a little uncomfortable with some of the comments about men," she admitted, her voice barely above a whisper. "I know it's not my place to say anything, and I don't want to sound ungrateful, but… it just felt a bit harsh. I guess I'm not used to it yet."

Evelyn's eyes softened, and she gave Clara's arm a gentle squeeze. "I understand," she said quietly. "It's easy to get caught up in the excitement of this new world, but it's important to remember that balance and empathy are still crucial. Thank you for being honest, Clara. Your perspective is valuable, and it's something we should all keep in mind."

Clara felt a wave of relief wash over her, the tension in her chest easing slightly. She nodded, offering a small, grateful smile. "Thank you, Evelyn. I really appreciate that." her shoulders relaxing just a fraction.

"So, it's really not a dream," Clara murmured. "We're *here*— wherever *here* is." She shook her head and exhaled, "But *how*? Magic? Science? A cosmic glitch?"

"Ask Nancy," Evelyn said, her eyes glinting with mischief as she nudged the woman beside her. "Our resident physics genius."

Nancy scoffed, swirling her whiskey before taking a slow sip. "*Former* physics teacher," she corrected, though there was no real bite to it. "But fine. If you want the textbook answer? Parallel universes. Quantum entanglement. Maybe your consciousness slipped into another version of you." She shrugged. "Or maybe the universe just has a twisted sense of humor."

Clara hesitated, then asked, "Do you think… there's another *me* living my old life right now?"

Nancy swirled her drink, considering. "Possible," she said finally. "If we're here, someone else could be there."

Evelyn let out a sharp laugh, shaking her head. "God, I pity her. Can you imagine another *me* trapped in that investment banking shark tank for 7 years?" Her voice softened, a shadow crossing her face. "All those boardroom battles, the way they'd talk over you like you weren't even there…" She met Clara's gaze, a wry smile tugging at her lips.

Clara blinked. She remembered— the old Evelyn's venting sessions, the eye rolls, the dark jokes. But it had never fully sunk in until now, watching this new Evelyn, freer and fiercer, speak of it with such quiet resignation. A pang of guilt twisted in her chest. *Had I even really listened back then?*

Clara's shoulders lifted in a slow, wordless shrug—a gesture that carried the weight of a thousand unspoken apologies. Her eyes met Evelyn's, and for the first time, she truly *saw* the exhaustion behind her friend's old stories—the late nights dismissed as "hysterical," the ideas stolen and repackaged by smirking colleagues, the way Evelyn's laughter in those days had always been a little too sharp, like glass cracking under pressure. *I should have listened harder,* Clara thought, her throat tightening. *I should have asked more questions.*

Then, like cold water rushing in, another realization seized her. "But what about their *Firen*?" she whispered, pressing a hand to her own chest as if she could still feel the phantom hum of that lost power. "If we're here in their world…, did they wake up in ours without it? Stripped of everything that made them strong?"

Nancy's gaze drifted to the window, where the street lights of this unfamiliar world hung low and luminous. She exhaled, long and slow, the sound carrying decades of quiet battles. "If the physics here bend differently…" Her calloused fingers tightened around her glass. "Then yes. They might be defenseless. Alone." A beat. Then, softer: "Or maybe they're learning to fight in new ways. Maybe they're surviving—like we did."

The silence between them wasn't empty; it thrummed with memory and possibility. Clara could almost taste it—the bitterness of regrets left behind, the metallic tang of hope not yet earned. *A second chance,* she thought, *but not a free one.*

She said to Nancy. "You seemed brilliant at teaching," Clara said, "Why leave the classroom?"

The question landed heavier than intended. Nancy's grip tightened around her glass, her gaze distant. "Because teaching doesn't pay the bills," she said quietly. "Not when the bank's threatening to take your mother's house. Not when the medical bills pile up and the insurance company weasels out of paying them." A bitter laugh escaped her. "So, I joined one. Climbed the ladder. Promised myself I'd build something better—a company that actually *helps* people instead of screwing them over." She met Clara's eyes, her voice raw. "Too late for my mom. But not too late for everyone else."

A weighted silence settled over them. Then Linda reached out, her hand warm over Nancy's. "Maybe that's why we're here," she said softly. "A second chance. A fresh start."

Evelyn lifted her glass, the golden liquid catching the light. "To the mess we left behind—and the future we're going to make."

One by one, their glasses clinked together, a quiet promise hanging in the air between them.

"To the mess and the future!" they all shouted, their voices echoing with a mix of triumph and resolve.

Clara's heart pounded as she stood in the center of the room, her mind racing with the weight of everything she had just heard. The air felt heavy, charged with an intensity that made her skin prickle. She glanced down at her hands, her unpolished nails suddenly feeling like a glaring vulnerability. Every woman in the room seemed to radiate power and confidence, their manicured nails glinting like weapons—symbols of their dominance in this new world. Clara's own hands felt bare, exposed, and she couldn't help but feel a pang of insecurity. She turned to Evelyn, her voice trembling slightly as she asked the question that had been gnawing at her since she arrived.

"May I ask… since we're from a different world originally, will my nails develop Firen too if I stay here long enough?"

The room fell into a deafening silence. It was as if the air had been sucked out of the space, leaving behind a vacuum of tension. Every pair of eyes snapped to Clara, their gazes sharp and probing, as though she had just uttered something forbidden, something dangerous. The weight of their stares pressed down on her, and for a moment, she felt like a deer caught in the headlights, frozen and vulnerable.

Emily was the first to break the silence, her voice firm and unyielding. "It's not going to happen to you."

Sarah stepped closer, her words measured but fierce. "Women from our world… we're different. The solar effect doesn't take us. But there's a catch." She held Clara's gaze, unflinching. "Even though, Firen typically does not get released until girls hit puberty, a female body either develops the foundation of Firen mechanism in the first three years of life, or she never will. The science is settled—70 years of research, countless studies. The system 'protects' non-Firen girls in special institutes, gives them benefits, treats them as disabled. But us? *We* don't exist in their records. We're ghosts."

A beat of silence. Then, quieter, lethal: "If they find out what you are, you won't be a person anymore. You'll be a specimen. A test subject. So, unless you *want* to spend the rest of your life under a microscope… you keep this to yourself."

The other women didn't blink, didn't move. Their stares burned into Clara—not just assessing, but *challenging*. *Prove you're one of us. Prove we can trust you.*

"All you need to do," Sarah continued, her voice dropping to a near whisper, "is keep your hands away from any man when you're angry. And never, 'ever' reveal this to anyone outside this room."

Clara felt her breath catch in her throat. The gravity of Sarah's words hit her like a tidal wave. Trying to process this shared hidden identity with the head of NYPD, Clara stood there, rooted to the spot, her mind racing with a mix of fear and disbelief. The room, once filled with laughter and camaraderie, now felt like a fortress of secrets, and Clara was suddenly acutely aware of how much she didn't know about this world.

Linda stepped forward, breaking the tension with a graceful smile. She extended her hands to Clara, her nails adorned with intricate designs that shimmered like tiny works of art. "Darling, look," she said, her voice soothing but firm. "If you decorate your nails like mine, men on the street will think you're just like every other powerful woman. And if you're polite to them—even if it's just because of your own insecurity—they'll appreciate it. They might even see you as a gentlewoman. Trust me, it could get you more boyfriends than you can imagine."

The room erupted into laughter, but Clara couldn't bring herself to join in. Her mind was still reeling, her emotions a tangled mess of fear, confusion, and a strange, almost giddy excitement. She felt overwhelmed, as though she had been thrust into a high-stakes game where the rules were still unclear.

Nancy's voice cut through the laughter, her tone sharp and serious. "Not if she meets those 'BLAND' kids."

The mood shifted instantly. The laughter died down, replaced by a tense silence. Clara's stomach churned as she looked around the room, her eyes wide with alarm. "What?" she asked, her voice barely above a whisper. "What are the 'BLAND' kids? Am I in danger?"

Evelyn sighed, her expression grim. "BLAND stands for the Boy-only Lands," she explained. "Decades ago, when Firen first emerged, men were terrified. Some of the wealthiest and most powerful men used their resources to create isolated territories—places where women weren't allowed. They stockpiled weapons, including nuclear warheads, and used them as a deterrent to keep women out. These territories became sanctuaries for men who were too afraid or too angry to live in a world dominated by women. They have their own governments, their own defense systems, and they're… hostile. Deeply hostile toward women."

Nancy nodded, her face serious. "They're essentially independent territories populated entirely by men. And unsurprisingly, their populations have been shrinking over the years. But don't let that fool you—they're still dangerous."

"Not always shrinking." Emily's voice was cold and steady, her military background evident in her tone, "There are always young men—angry, testosterone-fueled men—who snap under the fear of Firen and flee to the BLANDs. Some of them have threatened to nuke the Roses. We've caught spies sent from those territories. We can't afford to underestimate them."

The air in the room changed. Instead of the hum of confident voices, the clink of wine glasses, the warm glow of the antique chandeliers cast long shadows across the faces of the women around her, turning their determined expressions into something sharper. More dangerous.

A chill prickled the back of Clara's neck, raising the fine hairs along her arms. This wasn't just a meeting anymore. It was a war council.

Her mouth went dry. She swallowed hard, her throat tight. "Where are these territories?" she asked, her voice steadier than she felt. "Are any of them near NYC?"

Emily didn't answer right away. Instead, she flicked her wrist with a practiced motion, and a sleek, holographic display shot from her watch, expanding across the wall in a shimmer of light. Clara's breath caught. The contrast was jarring—this cutting-edge technology glowing against the faded opulence of the hotel's gilded wallpaper.

She stepped closer, her shoes sinking into the plush carpet as she studied the map. It was *wrong*. Not the geography she remembered from her old life, not the familiar contours of continents she had once known. This was something else entirely.

"The world is divided now," Emily said, her voice cool and precise. "The People's United Nations—our nation—controls ninety percent of the land and oceans. The rest…" She tapped the display, and a series of jagged red borders flickered to life, scattered like wounds across the map. "BLAND. Male extremists. They've carved out what they can."

Clara's eyes locked onto the marked territories—clusters of land north of the Indian Ocean, isolated, encircled by broken lines like quarantined zones. A shaky exhale escaped her. "So that's where they are," she murmured. "Far from here."

For a moment, relief washed over her. Distance meant safety. Didn't it?

But Sarah's next words shattered that fragile hope.

"They're far from our borders," she said, her tone grim. "But their influence isn't. We've been seeing more cases in the city—incidents, propaganda, whispers of their ideology spreading."

Clara's chest tightened. "What does that mean for me?" The question slipped out before she could stop it, her voice trembling just slightly.

Nancy's smirk was unsettling. "If they ever found out about women like us—women who don't generate Firen—they'd see us as a way to restore their dominance. They'd want to keep us, control us. And trust me, Clara, you don't want to know what that would look like."

"NO!" The word erupted from the women in unison, their voices sharp and forceful. Emily's expression was fierce as she turned to Nancy. "It's not a joke. Those men would take out their rage on us if they knew our nails were fake. Remember what happened two years ago? Those two drunk men from BLAND attacked that teenage girl after they realized her hands were covered in fiberglass gloves?"

Evelyn's voice was calm but firm as she addressed Clara. "Now you understand why you must never wear gloves in this world. They slow down the effect of Firen, and they... trigger something in some men. Something dark."

Clara felt her knees go weak. The room seemed to spin around her, the weight of the information pressing down on her chest. She had come here seeking a new beginning, a chance to thrive in a world that celebrated women. But now, she felt like she had stepped into a minefield, where every step carried the risk of danger.

Linda, who had been quietly observing from the corner, finally spoke up. Her voice was steady, a grounding presence in the midst of the chaos. "Clara, I know this is a lot to take in."

"The NYPD has your back. Just remember, the crime rate in this world is incredibly low, especially in cities like New York." Sarah added.

Linda nodded, her tone lighter now, though still tinged with caution. "And one more thing, the AI development here is more advanced than anything we had in our old world. There are AI cameras and crime identifiers at every street corner. I will give you our company's newly released AI watch that can put out siren and self-call the police once it detects that you are in danger. You're safe, Clara. But it's good to be aware."

Clara blinked rapidly, trying to process everything. She took a deep breath, her hands trembling as she clasped them together. The room seemed to come back into focus, the tension easing slightly as the women around her shifted back into their roles as mentors and allies.

Evelyn leaned forward, her eyes warm and encouraging. "Clara, we've shared a lot with you tonight. But now it's your turn. What's your passion? What sets your soul on fire?"

The question caught Clara off guard, pulling her out of the whirlwind of fear and uncertainty. For a moment, she hesitated, her mind still racing. But then, slowly, a spark of determination ignited within her. This world was complex, dangerous, and full of challenges—but it was also a world of opportunity, a world where she could finally pursue her dreams without apology.

Clara hesitated for a moment, her mind racing. She hadn't been asked that question in a long time—not in a way that felt genuine, at least. But here, surrounded by these resourceful women, she felt a spark of courage ignite within her. She looked around the room, meeting the eyes of each woman in turn. "Art," she said, her voice steadying as she spoke. "Creating something beautiful, something that speaks to people…it's where I feel most alive. But back in my old world, it was hard to make a living as an artist. I ended up putting it aside to focus on… well, surviving."

The women exchanged knowing glances, their smiles widening. "Art?" Linda said, her eyes lighting up. "That's incredible. The world always needs more beauty, more voices, more stories. And in the era of Roses, art isn't just a luxury—it's a necessity."

Sarah nodded enthusiastically. "Clara, you have no idea how much your talent could thrive here. The arts are celebrated, funded, and supported in ways you've probably never imagined. Women-run galleries, grants for female artists, mentorship programs—it's a whole ecosystem designed to uplift creators like you."

Emily leaned in, her sharp gaze softening. "And if you ever need a muse, the Navy's annual Christmas party is a goldmine of inspiration," she said with a wink, earning a round of laughter from the group.

Nancy's warm smile was reassuring. "If you're serious about restarting your life in fine art, I can connect you with some incredible resources. My company sponsors a number of initiatives that support women in the arts, from funding to exhibition opportunities. You wouldn't be starting from scratch—you'd have a whole network behind you."

Linda's eyes sparkled with excitement. "And if you're interested in merging art with technology, LindAI Media has a division dedicated to digital art and immersive experiences. We're always looking for fresh talent to collaborate with. Imagine your work being showcased in virtual galleries or integrated into AI-driven storytelling. The possibilities are endless."

Evelyn placed a hand on Clara's arm, her touch grounding and reassuring. "Clara, this is your moment. You've been given a second chance in a world that values your creativity and your voice. Let us help you take that first step."

Clara felt a lump rise in her throat, her eyes welling with tears. For the first time in years, she felt seen, heard, and truly supported. "I… I don't know what to say," she stammered, her voice trembling with emotion. "This is more than I ever dreamed of. Thank you."

"No need to thank me yet," Evelyn said with a sly smile, her eyes glinting with a mix of warmth and mischief. "We've all been through the shock of being transported into this parallel universe. I know exactly how you feel—disoriented, amazed, maybe even a little terrified. But here's the thing: we're in this together. We stick together, we help each other, and we rise together." She paused, her gaze sweeping across the room, as if sharing a secret only they could understand. "And speaking of secrets… our little group has a name. A "secret" name. We call ourselves ROWFIR—Roses Without Firen."

The room seemed to hold its breath as Evelyn reached for a sleek, crystal glass filled with deep red wine. She held it out to Clara, the liquid catching the light like liquid rubies. "Once you drink this, you'll officially be one of us. A Rose Without Firen. So, Clara… are you ready to join the sisterhood?"

Clara's heart raced, her eyes widening with a mix of excitement and curiosity. The air felt electric, charged with the weight of the moment. She reached for the glass, her fingers trembling slightly as she wrapped them around the stem. The women around the table leaned in, their eyes locked on her, their expressions a blend of anticipation and pride.

Clara took a deep breath, "I'm ready." Her voice steady despite the whirlwind of emotions inside her. She raised the glass, her smile widening as she met the gaze of each woman in the room.

The women erupted into cheers, their applause filling the space like a thunderous wave. Glasses clinked, laughter rang out, and the energy in the room was nothing short of intoxicating. Linda stood, her glass raised high, her voice cutting through the noise like a clarion call. "May her art light up the world and inspire generations to come! To Clara!" She declared, her eyes sparkling with excitement.

"To Clara!" the others echoed, their voices harmonizing into a powerful chorus of empowerment and solidarity. The sound was electric, sending shivers down Clara's spine. She felt a surge of belonging, of being part of something bigger than herself—something extraordinary.

With a deep breath, Clara brought the glass to her lips and drank. The wine was rich and velvety, its warmth spreading through her like a promise. As she lowered the glass, the women erupted into another round of cheers, their enthusiasm infectious.

"Bottoms up!" someone shouted, and the room filled with laughter and the sound of glasses being drained. Clara couldn't help but laugh too, her heart swelling with a sense of camaraderie and possibility. She had stepped into a world of secrets, power, and sisterhood—and she was ready to embrace it all.

As the celebration continued, Clara felt a thrill of excitement coursing through her veins. She was no longer just a newcomer in this strange, dazzling world. She was a Rose Without Firen—a woman with a secret, a purpose, and a sisterhood that would stand by her side no matter what. And as she looked around the room at the faces of these extraordinary women, she knew one thing for certain: her life was about to become more thrilling, more mysterious, and more extraordinary than she had ever imagined.

As the night wore on, the conversation flowed effortlessly, each woman sharing stories of their own journeys and offering Clara advice, connections, and encouragement. Sarah talked about the power of art in community building, while Emily shared how creativity had been her anchor during her toughest moments in the military. Nancy spoke about the healing power of art and its role in mental health, and Linda painted a vivid picture of the future of art in the digital age. Evelyn, ever the strategist, helped Clara outline a plan to relaunch her career, from securing studio space to building a portfolio that would turn heads.

By the time Clara left the Beekwomen Hotel, her heart was full, and her mind was buzzing with ideas. The city skyline glittered like a canvas waiting to be painted, and for the first time in what felt like forever, Clara felt like she was exactly where she was meant to be.

As she walked through the cool night air, she couldn't help but smile. This wasn't just a new beginning—it was a rebirth. With the support of these incredible women and the resources they had offered, Clara knew she was ready to reclaim her passion and make her mark on the world.

She pulled out her phone and opened a blank note, her fingers flying across the screen as she jotted down ideas for her first project. A series of paintings celebrating the strength and resilience of women, perhaps. Or a sculpture that captured the essence of the era of Roses. The possibilities were endless, and for the first time in years, Clara felt truly alive.

As she reached her apartment, she paused at the door, taking a deep breath. "This is it," she whispered to herself. "This is where it all begins."

And with that, Clara stepped inside, ready to paint her future in bold, vibrant strokes. The era of Roses had given her a second chance, and she was determined to make it count.

CHAPTER 6: CATERING STAFF

On July 18, 2027, Clara's face—and her gallery's stunning artwork—lit up Times Square, flashing across the giant screens every hour for 15 glorious seconds. For one unforgettable day, New York City paused, looked up, and saw her vision shining brighter than the skyline.

Two years had passed since Clara found herself thrust into a world where women ruled and men navigated a society that mirrored the struggles she once faced. In that time, she had built an empire—a thriving art gallery and auction business that had become the talk of New York City. Her name was now synonymous with innovation, creativity, and success. Yet, despite her achievements, Clara's journey was far from simple.

Clara's art gallery, *Era of Roses*, was more than just a gallery—it was a sanctuary of beauty, creativity, and sophistication. Nestled in the vibrant heart of Manhattan, the space was a stunning fusion of modern elegance and timeless artistry, designed to captivate and inspire at every turn. The walls were a canvas of expression, adorned with an exquisite collection of works from both established masters and rising talents, each piece thoughtfully curated to weave a narrative that resonated with the soul. Every corner of the gallery exuded an atmosphere of refinement and grace, offering visitors an immersive experience in the world of art.

Clara had turned her gallery into an exclusive cultural hub, where every event was a celebration of creativity. Her auctions, renowned for their grandeur and allure, had become highly anticipated occasions, drawing the attention of Hollywood icons, influential billionaires, and passionate art collectors from every corner of the globe. These glamorous gatherings were not just about acquiring masterpieces; they were an opportunity to be part of an elite circle, a chance to experience the rare intersection of art, luxury, and innovation.

Over the last two years, Clara had sold pieces to A-list celebrities and powerful figures, solidifying her place as one of the most influential curators in the art world. Her keen eye for emerging talent and her deep appreciation for timeless beauty had earned her the reputation of a cultural icon—an authority whose gallery was a must-visit destination for those seeking to experience art in its most captivating and inspiring forms.

Moreover, Clara's success was never just about the art—it was about crafting an experience that left a lasting impression. She knew that true luxury wasn't just found in the pieces on the walls, but in the moments that surrounded them. That's why she hosted exclusive fundraising events at some of New York City's most opulent hotels, places that exuded glamour and refinement at every turn. These events were much more than fundraisers—they were curated celebrations of creativity, filled with stunning details that captivated the senses.

Partnering with Linda's media company, Clara ensured that each event was flawlessly executed, creating an atmosphere that felt both elegant and effortless. Guests were treated to exquisite catering, with carefully selected dishes designed to delight the palate, while live performances added a layer of enchantment to the evening. The entire event felt like stepping into a world of sophistication, where every detail had been thoughtfully crafted to evoke awe and inspiration.

On a crisp, invigorating October evening in New York, the city seemed to hum with a quiet magic. The air was cool and fresh, carrying the faint scent of fallen leaves and distant woodsmoke. The sky above was a deep, velvety blue, dotted with the first twinkling stars of the night. The streets were alive with the soft glow of streetlights, their golden beams reflecting off the polished surfaces of skyscrapers and the occasional puddle left by an afternoon rain. It was the kind of night that made you want to wrap yourself in a cozy scarf, breathe in deeply, and savor the feeling of being alive in a city that never slept but somehow felt still, just for a moment. The kind of night that whispered promises of warmth, connection, and the gentle thrill of something beautiful about to unfold.

The grand ballroom of the Beekwomen Hotel was alive with energy. Crystal chandeliers cast a soft glow over the room, their light reflecting off the polished marble floors. The air was filled with the hum of conversation, the clinking of glasses, and the occasional burst of laughter. It was one of Clara's signature art auction events, and the room was packed with New York's elite —art collectors, Hollywood stars, and influential figures from across the country.

One of the most unforgettable aspects of Clara's events was the catering staff. While most people's eyes were drawn to the art, the elegant décor, and the stunning guest list, there was one detail that never failed to catch the attention of those fortunate enough to attend her exclusive gatherings: the strikingly handsome young men who worked the events. The staff wasn't just about serving cocktails or arranging hors d'oeuvres—they were part of the sophisticated ambiance Clara had so carefully curated. Their presence, along with their impeccable manners and professional demeanor, brought an undeniable energy to each event, making them a crucial element in creating a memorable experience.

What made Clara's catering staff even more interesting was the diversity of their backgrounds and ambitions. Some were full-time catering professionals, having honed their skills through years of training in the art of fine dining and event execution.

They had perfected the art of moving with grace, presenting food as if it were a masterpiece in itself, and knowing just when to step forward with a smile, offering guests what they needed without ever being intrusive. These men understood the delicate balance between service and sophistication, and they played their roles to perfection, elevating the atmosphere of every event they were part of.

But it wasn't just the seasoned professionals who stood out. Among the staff, there were also many part-timers—young men working their way through the unpredictable world of the arts and entertainment. Some dreamed of becoming actors, others wanted to break into the world of fashion, and a few had aspirations in music or photography. They were talented, driven, and full of ambition, and yet, they were still finding their way. Their paths were fraught with obstacles, not just because of their chosen industries, but because of the reality of being men in fields where women often held the reins of power.

Clara moved through the crowd with practiced ease, her elegant navy-blue nails shinning as she greeted guests with a warm smile. She was in her element, but her attention was drawn to a man standing near the edge of the room. He was part of the catering team. His crisp white shirt and black bow tie a stark contrast to the vibrant energy of the event. His makeup is flawlessly applied, enhancing his youthful appearance and giving him an undeniably charming and adorable look. It's clear that men today have mastered the art of makeup, using it to their advantage in ways that highlight their best features. Many men opt for makeup techniques that make them appear younger and more innocent, knowing that this look is especially appealing to women. The subtlety and skill involved in their choices create an attractive, fresh-faced vibe, one that resonates with women who find this youthful innocence incredibly captivating.

What truly caught Clara's attention, however, was the way he stood by the artwork, almost as though he were mesmerized by it. He seemed to be lost in the colors, the shapes, the emotions. His gaze remained fixed on a particular abstract piece, one that seemed to speak to him in ways that words could not. To an outsider, it might have just appeared as a collection of swirling shapes and bold strokes, but to Clara, it evoked a powerful story—one of raw passion, vulnerability, and longing.

The painting, with its vivid hues and contrasting tones, struck her deeply. It was a depiction of what seemed to be two figures—abstracted, yet somehow deeply intimate. Clara, ever the romantic, couldn't help but imagine it as a metaphor for love. She saw it as two men, caught in a moment of pure emotion, kissing a rose as though it were the most precious thing in the world—yet their tears betrayed a deeper sadness, a sorrow they couldn't quite hide. It was the kind of image that tugged at her heart, the kind that made you think of unspoken desires and unfulfilled dreams.

What intrigued her most, though, was the way he looked at the painting. His eyes softened, the corners of his mouth twitching in a small, almost imperceptible smile. There was something vulnerable in his expression, as if he too saw the depth in the piece—the tenderness, the longing. It was clear that this artwork had reached him in a way that no one else in the room seemed to notice. His body language was almost reverential, as if he were standing before something sacred.

Clara felt a sudden curiosity. She knew there was a story behind his gaze, a story that he wasn't ready to share with anyone yet. Maybe it was the way the painting reminded him of a love lost or a passion he couldn't fully express. Or perhaps, like her, he simply saw beauty in the pain—how often do we look at art and find ourselves reflected in its strokes and colors?

The longer she watched him, the more Clara realized how much she admired his ability to connect with the artwork on such a deep level. It was a reminder to her of how often people move through life, distracted and detached from the emotions that truly matter. But here he was, fully engaged with the piece, feeling every emotion it stirred. It was the kind of attention that Clara, with her own love for art and beauty, could appreciate.

For a moment, the gallery around her seemed to fade away. It was just the two of them, caught in the quiet intimacy of art and the unspoken understanding between them. The painting, which had already captured Clara's heart, had now become a symbol of something much more. It was a link between her and him, something they both silently shared—an appreciation for the quiet, powerful beauty in the world around them.

She approached him, her curiosity piqued. "That's one of my favorites," she said, gesturing to the painting. "What do you think of it?"

The young man turned, startled but polite. "Oh, I—I think it's incredible," he stammered, his voice soft but earnest. "The way the colors blend, it's like… it's like the artist is telling a story without words."

Clara smiled, intrigued. "You have a good eye. What's your name?"

"Ethan," he replied, extending his hand. "Ethan Carter. It's an honor to meet you, Ms. Rose. I've been following your work for a while now."

Clara is pleased, noting the sincerity in his eyes. "Please, call me Clara. And the honor is mine. It's great to see an inspired youth who appreciates art as much as you seem to."

Ethan kept his hands clasped behind his back. His shoulders slightly rounded as if trying to take up less space. When he spoke, his voice was soft, hesitant—the kind of tone one uses when afraid of saying too much.

Clara thought it would be helpful to gather a fresh mind for her work. She asked, "Any other display here that caught your eyes?"

"Um, like this one." he gesturing timidly toward the paintings of women in power. His fingers barely lifted before retreating again, as if he wasn't sure he had the right to point. "The women are almost always middle-aged, looking down or gazing far away—untouchable, powerful, but distant. But the men..." He trailed off, his gaze dropping to a smaller painting of a young father holding a baby, admiring his wife with adoring eyes." Men are shown as nurturers. As if their greatest purpose is to love, support, and care... but never to lead."

Ethan seemed too insecure to continue. His voice cracked slightly, and Clara felt an unexpected pang of recognition. *This was how many women felt in her old world.*

"You've got a point," she admitted softly, as if seeing her own past self in his frustration.

Ethan looked up at her and seemed to found some hope. "I don't... I don't mean to complain—I'd love a family one day. But it's like society is telling us that's all we're good for. Sometimes it feels like the only story they want us to have is about...belonging to someone else. That our dreams, our ambitions, should always come second." He it his lip, glancing at Clara as if waiting for her to judge him.

"That's a very good point." Clara felt a strong irony. How many times had she swallowed her own thoughts like this long time ago in a different world. "Are there other things here that bother you?"

He nodded, his fingers nervously tracing the edge of his sleeve. "There's... there's more, if you... if you want to see."

He led her to a display of men's hair products, his steps hesitant. The boxes showed impossibly handsome men, their hair gleaming under studio lights. Ethan pointed at a dye box, his hand slightly shaking, his voice barely above a whisper.

"For example, these ads—perfect, chiseled male models with flawless curls, promising every guy he can look like this if he just buys the right product. They make it look so easy. But once you start... it's like you can't stop. Your hair gets brittle, and then...

then they sell you something else like a 'hair restorative serums' to fix it. And when that doesn't work..." He held his hands together, as if afraid of being scolded for touching it. "Well. There's always another wig shop on the 5th Ave, I suppose."

There was no bitterness in his voice—just resignation. As if this was simply the way things were, and fighting it would be pointless.

Clara felt refreshed by the clear address on the diabolical side of business model. Ethan's mind was not surprising but still intriguing enough to Clara.

Just then, the TV in the corner of the room flickered to a documentary dissecting *"The Art of Filming Male Victims in Rape Scenes."* Ethan stiffened. On screen, a director explained how to best capture "the raw terror in a man's eyes".

"I like your mindset. How do you feel about the documentary?" Clara asked.

"I know these are supposed to be... important stories," he murmured, his eyes fixed on the floor. "But the way they film us... it's like they want you to 'see' us break. Women get shadows, but men... men get close-ups." His voice cracked, just slightly. "It's not... it's not fair."

The admission seemed to cost him something. He shrunk in on himself, as if bracing for a reprimand.

Clara's heart twisted. "You're right," she said softly. "It's not fair at all."

Ethan looked up, surprised, as if kindness was the last thing he'd expected. "Yes, by fetishizing male suffering. The camera lingers on our fear, our shame—like it's for entertainment. Real victims deserve dignity, not...this. Honestly, I... I'd like to make better stories one day. I want to make films that treat men with respect. That show our pain without exploiting it." he seemed determined and inspired. But soon, he looks down and in almost whispering, "If... if anyone would let me."

Clara wanted to tell him he 'would', that he 'could'—but the words stuck in her throat. Because she knew, in this world, how unlikely that was.

And so instead, she simply said, "I hope you do."

Ethan gave her a small, fragile smile—the kind that looked like it was used to being crushed. "Thank you," he said, so quietly she almost missed it. "That's… that's very kind of you."

And as he turned away, shoulders hunched against the weight of a world that had already decided his place, Clara realized with a chill:

"This wasn't just a different world."

"It was a mirror."

As the evening wore on, Clara learned that he was 20 years old, a student at NYU studying art history. His family, he explained, had a long tradition of education—his mother was a professor of neuroscience at Columbia University, and his father, though now a stay-at-home dad, had once been a popular music teacher at a private elementary school. Ethan spoke with a quiet pride about his family, even though his mother always wanted to have a daughter instead a son and almost had a divorce after his father was diagnosed with infertility and depression after working too hard as a stay-home dad. There was a hint of anger and sadness in his voice when he talked about his own aspirations.

"I've always loved art," he said, his eyes lighting up. "I used to spend hours in museums when I was a kid, just… absorbing everything. I wanted to be an artist, but…" He trailed off, his gaze dropping to the floor.

"But?" Clara prompted gently.

Ethan sighed. "It's so hard. In this world, it constantly feels like the odds are stacked against men. I've applied for internships, submitted my work to all kinds of content designing companies, or traditional galleries but… it's like no one takes me seriously. I'm just a 'pretty boy' to the industries."

Clara's heart ached at his words. She recognized the frustration in his voice, the same frustration she had felt in her old world. "I understand," she said softly. "It's not easy to break into an industry that doesn't always see your potential. But that doesn't mean you should give up."

As they talked, Clara learned more about Ethan's talent. He showed her photos of his work on his phone—vivid, emotive pieces that spoke of a deep understanding of color and form. His art was raw and honest, a reflection of his struggles and dreams. Clara was impressed. "Ethan, these are incredible," she said, her voice filled with genuine admiration. "You have a real gift."

Ethan blushed, clearly unused to such praise. "Thank you," he murmured. "It means a lot coming from you."

Clara's mind raced with possibilities. She knew how difficult it was for young men like Ethan to find opportunities in the arts, but she also knew she had the power to change that. "Listen," she said, her tone firm but kind. "I'd love to feature your work in my gallery. We could do a small exhibition, give you a platform to showcase your talent. What do you think?"

Ethan's eyes widened in disbelief. "Are you serious? That would be… incredible. But why would you do that for me?"

Clara smiled. Her gaze steady. "Because I see myself in you. I know what it's like to feel invisible, to fight for a chance to prove yourself. And I believe in paying it forward. You have a gift, Ethan, and the world deserves to see it."

As the event began to wind down, the ballroom grew quieter, the hum of conversation softening into a gentle murmur. Clara and Ethan remained in their corner, their dialogue flowing as effortlessly as a quiet river under the moonlight. They spoke of art, its power to heal and inspire, and of life's unpredictable twists and turns. Ethan, who had initially been reserved, now seemed more at ease, his laughter warm and his eyes bright with the kind of hope only a dreamer could possess. Clara, in turn, found herself quietly charmed by his earnestness, his polite demeanor, and the way his passion for art mirrored her own.

Yet, as much as she wanted to open up to him, to share the weight of her own struggles—the insecurities she had carried like a shadow, the battles she had fought to rise above a world that once dismissed her—she held back. Her past was a locked box, sealed with a promise she had made to herself and to the secret society of ROWFIR. She had learned to adapt, to polish her nails with the same meticulous care as the women of Firen, to blend seamlessly into this world of power and privilege. But beneath the surface, her heart ached with the memories of a life where she had been the one overlooked, the one fighting to be seen.

She watched Ethan as he spoke, his hands gesturing animatedly, his voice filled with a youthful optimism that tugged at her heart. There was a part of her that longed to tell him everything—to let him know that she understood his struggles more deeply than he could imagine. But she couldn't. Not yet. Not without breaking the promise she had made to herself and to the women who had welcomed her into their world.

Instead, she listened, her silence a quiet testament to the empathy she felt for him. She admired his resilience, his determination to chase his dreams despite the odds stacked against him. And though she couldn't share her own story, she made a silent vow to help him in whatever way she could—to be the mentor she had never had, the guiding light in a world that often felt too dark for dreamers like him.

By the end of the night, Clara had not only offered Ethan a chance to showcase his work but had also become a mentor and friend. She gave him her card, urging him to reach out whenever he needed advice or support. "This is just the beginning, Ethan," she said as they parted ways. "Don't let anyone tell you that your dreams aren't worth pursuing."

Ethan nodded, his eyes shining with gratitude. "Thank you, Clara. I won't let you down."

"I know you won't," Clara said with a warm smile. "Enjoy the rest of your night."

Ethan grinned, his face lighting up with pure joy, looking like the happiest kid on earth. "This is the best night of my life," he said, his voice filled with excitement. "I'll never forget it."

As Clara watched him walk away, her heart felt a mix of warmth and sympathy. She knew the road ahead wouldn't be easy for him, but she also saw something extraordinary in him—a spark that was hard to ignore. Standing there alone, in the soft, fading glow of the evening, she allowed herself a quiet moment of vulnerability. Her polished nails shimmered in the dim light, a reflection of the world she now found herself in—a world full of secrets, but one she had grown into with grace.

Despite her remarkable achievements, Clara often carried a quiet undercurrent of insecurity. She had always been a relentless worker, but in this new world, she pushed herself to the edge, her days a whirlwind of meetings, events, and creative decisions. Rarely did she allow herself a moment to pause, driven by a gnawing fear that it could all vanish—that one day, she might wake up back in her old world, stripped of the resources and opportunities she now cherished. This fear, while grounding, also haunted her. She frequently found herself reflecting on her past life, the struggles she had endured, and the person she had once been. Those memories were a stark reminder of how swiftly the world could shift, fueling her determination to seize every moment in her current reality. Yet, they also left her feeling like an outsider, as though she didn't fully belong in this world of powerful women and evolving dynamics.

Under ROWFIR's support, Clara's success was undeniable, but when she encountered the vulnerability in young men like

Ethan, something profound stirred within her. In a society where women dominated industries like entertainment and the arts, she saw how these young men were fighting a different kind of battle. Once, gender bias had worked against women in fields like business and law; now, men faced their own set of challenges in creative industries. Despite the glamour and influence of the entertainment world, it was largely controlled by female gatekeepers—women who held the keys to casting, sponsorships, and networking. The art world, too, had transformed, with women occupying influential roles as curators, critics, and artists. This shift left many young men, brimming with talent and ambition, feeling overlooked and undervalued.

For these men, no matter how gifted or driven they were, opportunities often seemed just out of reach. Some worked tirelessly to gain recognition, only to face rejection or condescension. Others found the constant struggle to break through in a female-dominated world to be an insurmountable hurdle. Adding to their frustration was the societal expectation that, once successful, many men would transition into roles as full-time fathers after having children. This wasn't just because they often earned less than their wives, but also because society viewed them as better suited for domestic responsibilities.

While women blessed with Firen were lauded for their razor-sharp intellect, their genius for strategic foresight, and their innate command in leadership roles, men carved their value from a different, more elemental foundation. They were the anchors of physicality in a household, prized for their formidable muscle strength and their unflinching endurance in handling life's grueling labors. Their presence was a cornerstone of domestic harmony; they could move through the intricate web of family relationships with a safe and steadying grace, their calm demeanor often acting as a balm to soothe daily tensions and instill a profound sense of stability.

This was a stability built not just on emotion, but on

sheer physical capability. Their natural propensity for muscle endurance made them uniquely suited for the tedious yet vital tasks that formed the backbone of a functioning home. They were the ones who could heave a heavy sofa to vacuum the dust bunnies lurking beneath, their biceps straining with the effort. They were the figures under the sink, patiently diagnosing the leaky pipe with grease-smudged hands, or spending long hours in the garage, resurrecting a broken appliance through sheer force of will and practical know-how. Their role extended through the night, where they were the patient guardians who could stay awake into the small hours, soothing a feverish child or attending to the restless needs of an elderly parent.

And though the silent, efficient hum of AI workers now managed more of these burdens—with mechanical arms that never tired and algorithms that never needed sleep—men remained indispensable. They were not replaced, but rather evolved into major players whose value transcended mere brute force, becoming a cherished and resilient constant in the heart of every household.

For many men, this role as the backbone of the household was a source of pride. They took on the responsibility of managing the home with dedication, ensuring that their families were cared for and their lives ran seamlessly. Yet, as the years passed, a quiet reality began to settle in. After spending several years as full-time house husbands, many of these men found themselves at a crossroads. The skills they had honed—patience, organization, and physical endurance—were invaluable within the home, but they didn't always translate to the professional world. When they attempted to re-enter the workforce, they often faced an uphill battle.

The jobs available to them were typically lower-paying and offered limited opportunities for advancement. Positions in caregiving, manual labor, or entry-level service roles were often the only options, and even then, competition was fierce. Many employers viewed their years spent at home as a gap in their professional experience, rather than recognizing the immense value of the skills they had developed. The societal expectation that men were better suited for domestic roles further compounded the issue, creating a cycle that was difficult to break.

For Clara observing this dynamic, it was impossible not to feel a pang of empathy. These men, who had dedicated themselves to their families with such unwavering commitment, now found themselves struggling to find their place in a world that seemed to have moved on without them. It was a stark reminder of the challenges women had faced in the old world, where their contributions were often undervalued and their potential overlooked. Now, the tables had turned, and the struggles of these men resonated deeply with women who had once walked a similar path.

Having endured her own struggles before, Clara understood the importance of lifting others up in a world that often felt more competitive than cooperative. She saw potential in these young men—not just as catering staff at her events, but as individuals with the talent and drive to make a meaningful impact.

Over the last two years, Clara consciously ran her business in a way that was inclusive and welcoming to men. She offered roles that went beyond entry-level positions, mentored aspiring male artists, and even featured their work in her gallery. While these gestures might have seemed small, they were significant steps toward creating a more balanced and equitable world. In this new chapter of her life, Clara wasn't just focused on climbing to the top—she was determined to bring others with her. For her, true success was measured not by individual achievement, but by the ability to uplift and empower those around her.

Nevertheless, one of the most refreshing aspects of Clara's new life was the sense of sisterhood she had found among the women in her circle. These were women who celebrated each other's successes without much jealousy or competition, who offered support and guidance without hesitation. It was a stark contrast to the cutthroat environment she had known in her old world. Here, collaboration was valued over competition, and women lifted each other up with genuine warmth.

But while women thrived with all kinds of supporting networks, men faced a different reality. The competition among them was fierce, fueled by limited opportunities and societal expectations. Many men struggled with feelings of inadequacy and frustration. Clara had become acutely aware of these dynamics. She had seen the jealousy that simmered among men, the way they competed for the few opportunities available to them. In short, *men were mean. Men were mean towards men*. It was a reflection of the struggles women had faced in her old world, and it left her feeling conflicted. She wanted to help, but she knew it wasn't a battle she could fight alone.

Since the conversation with Ethan, Clara felt her journey was about more than personal success—it was about creating a legacy of empathy, inclusion, and shared opportunity. She had established herself in the world, and now, she was determined to use her influence to make that world a little brighter for others. And in doing so, she found a deeper sense of purpose, one that transcended the glittering surface of her achievements and touched the very heart of what it meant to truly succeed.

CHAPTER 7: DADA FOR DADA

After their wonderful first meeting, Clara quickly recognized Ethan's potential and hired him as her assistant. From the start, she was impressed by his incredible work ethic and natural talent. Ethan's keen eye for art was unmatched—every piece he selected for the gallery perfectly aligned with Clara's vision, bringing a fresh energy to the space. Beyond his artistic skills, Ethan's sweet and patient nature shone through in every event he helped organize. His ability to manage the details with grace and charm made him an indispensable part of Clara's team, and she couldn't have been more pleased with their growing collaboration.

One afternoon, as Clara oversaw the preparations for an upcoming community event, she noticed something that piqued her curiosity. James, one of her part-time catering staff, had just set down a heavy box of utensils and was now furiously typing on his phone, his brow furrowed in concentration. There was a sense of urgency in his movements, as though he were juggling a dozen tasks at once. Clara watched him for a moment, her interest growing. What could be so important that it demanded his attention in the middle of a busy workday?

Ethan had just returned from running a few errands for the event and was now organizing a stack of invoices nearby. He noticed Clara's gaze on James. "James must be busy with his family errands again," Ethan remarked.

Clara turned to Ethan. Her concern evident. "Do you know what's going on? Is everything okay with him?"

Ethan hesitated, then sighed softly. "I'm not entirely sure, but I know his wife just had a baby. She's still in the 'rosy month care' period, and James took out a postpartum debt to hire a certified postpartum worker to help out. Money's tight for them right now. It's tough, but he's doing everything he can to make it work."

Clara's eyes widened. "The 'rosy month care'? What's that?"

Ethan nodded, clearly used to explaining this to someone unfamiliar with the concept. "It's a special healthcare period for women during the first month after childbirth. The idea is that the mom stays in bed as much as possible to recover, while a certified postpartum worker takes care of the newborn and helps with the mom's daily needs. They're really well-trained—they even teach the new dad how to care for the baby so he can adjust to his new role. People call it the 'rosy month care' because it's supposed to be this beautiful, nurturing time for the family."

Clara's expression softened. "That sounds incredibly helpful. I can see why it's so important."

"It is," Ethan agreed, "but it's also really expensive. Not every family can afford it, even though doctors highly recommend it. James took out a postpartum debt to cover the costs because he wants the best care for his wife. He's really dedicated to making sure she's comfortable and supported."

Clara tilted her head, intrigued. "A postpartum debt? I've heard of that before. Is it hard to get?"

"Not at all," Ethan replied. "It's actually part of the social welfare system now, so it's easy to apply for. But it can take a long time for husbands to pay it back, especially if they're not earning much."

Clara frowned, her curiosity deepening. "Why doesn't the wife help pay it off if she makes more money? Wouldn't that make sense?"

Ethan shrugged. "Some wives do help, but the social norm—at least here in NYC—is that a decent dad should cover the cost. Women already make such a huge contribution with their bodies during pregnancy, so it's seen as the husband's responsibility to handle the postpartum care. In some parts of the South, it's even more intense. Husbands are expected to not only cover the rosy month care but also give their wives a significant amount of money when they get married. It's like compensation for the wife's role in financially supporting the husband later on, especially since most men don't earn much after becoming househusbands."

Clara felt a pang of empathy as she processed this. The weight of these expectations on men—especially new fathers—was both fascinating and heartbreaking. "I see," she said quietly, her mind racing. "How do you know so much about all this, Ethan? You seem a little young to be so well-versed in family dynamics."

Ethan chuckled softly. "My cousin just had a baby eight months ago. He's in the exact same situation as James. I've seen how hard it can be."

"I see," Clara said, her tone softening. "Thanks for explaining all this to me, Ethan. It's really eye-opening."

As soon as the words left her mouth, Clara felt a flicker of nervousness. She realized she might have come across as strangely uninformed about the social norms of this world. Did Ethan suspect that she wasn't from here? She quickly tried to cover her tracks, adopting a playful tone. "Do you find it surprising that I didn't know these things?"

Ethan shook his head, his expression reassuring. "No, not at all. I remember you told me you're from Canada. I've heard Canadians are generally more egalitarian, with better healthcare and a more balanced approach to family life. Things must be different there."

His response eased Clara's nerves. Ethan's willingness to accept her inquiry without suspicion was a relief, and she felt a surge of gratitude for his sharing of information and thoughts. After he left to run more errands, Clara's attention returned to James, who had finally put his phone away and was now lifting the heavy box of utensils onto his shoulder. As he walked across the room, his movements steady despite the weight he carried, Clara felt an overwhelming urge to talk to him.

Clara moved gracefully through the bustling event space, her designer flat heels clicking softly against the polished concrete floor. The hum of caterers preparing for the evening's gala faded into background noise as she approached James, who was carefully arranging silverware at one of the VIP tables.

She paused a respectful distance away, watching as he wiped his brow with the back of his hand before speaking. "James," she said gently, her voice warm with concern, "could I ask you something?"

He startled slightly, nearly dropping the fork he was holding before turning to face her. His face was a canvas of exhaustion and quiet stress—the kind she recognized in working fathers who balanced duty and survival. "Of course, Ms. Rose," he replied automatically, straightening into that deferential posture employees adopted around management.

Clara hesitated, choosing her words carefully. "I couldn't help but notice you seemed preoccupied earlier with your phone. Is everything okay?"

James paled slightly, his fingers twisting the edge of his apron. "Oh, I'm so sorry, Ms. Rose. I didn't mean to check my phone during work hours—"

She waved a hand, her silver vintage watch catching the light. "No, no, it's fine. Ethan mentioned your wife just had a baby. I understand you've got a lot on your plate."

His shoulders relaxed slightly, and for the first time, Clara saw past the professional mask—the proud but exhausted father beneath. "Thanks, Ms. Rose," he admitted, voice softening. "It's… a lot. But we're managing. My wife's recovering well, and the baby—" His face transformed, a tired but radiant smile breaking through. "She's perfect. Healthy. That's what matters."

Clara felt an unexpected tightness in her chest. The way his eyes lit up despite the fatigue reminded her of something precious—her own father, years ago, his hands steady as he taught her to ride a bike.

"You're doing an incredible job, James," she said sincerely. "If there's anything I can do to help—extra shifts, flexibility—just ask."

His gratitude was palpable. "That means more than you know." He hesitated, then added, "Actually… I was messaging another dad from our support group. We trade baby items to help each other out."

Clara tilted her head, intrigued. "A support group?"

James' face brightened. "DADA for DADA. It's a network for full-time dads. We share advice, resources…" He chuckled. "Last week, one guy finally mastered the perfect swaddle after three months. We celebrated like he'd won gold."

Clara smiled, genuinely touched by James' reaction. But then his expression shifted, his voice lowering. "Two boys already, and now our little girl. I'm actually considered as very experienced and established in the dads' community. And…" he paused a second before continued, "my in-laws finally started to show a little bit respect towards me now that she was born."

Clara's stomach tightened. "Did you feel mistreated by them before?"

James shook his head quickly. "No, I'm lucky. Some of my wife's cousins… their parents weren't as patient. A few guys got divorced for only having sons. One even had to accept his wife taking a second husband."

The words hit Clara like a physical blow. She studied James—the tremor in his hands, the way his eyes darted to his phone for updates—and saw not just an employee, but a man navigating a world rigid and unfair. She noticed how his voice softened only when speaking of his daughter.

"I get why it's important to have daughters in the family. Unlike boys who are difficult and clumsy. My baby girl is sweet and bright. She'll look after me when I'm old," he said with quiet reverence. The unspoken contrast hung between them: sons were burdens; daughters were retirement plans.

A shiver traced Clara's spine. The painful symmetry was undeniable. Just as women in her old world had contorted themselves to fit expectations, these men had internalized their roles so completely that they accepted emotional—even physical—abuse as "women exercising leadership." Male assertiveness was "rudeness"; female bluntness was "strength."

Around them, young male servers moved with practiced neutrality. Clara wondered how many hid similar struggles behind polite smiles.

"Ms. Rose?" James' tentative voice pulled her back. "Was there anything else you needed?"

Clara blinked, forcing a polished smile. "No, James. Thank you for sharing your thoughts with me."

As he returned to work, she turned to the floor-to-ceiling windows, staring at her reflection superimposed over the glittering skyline. The woman looking back wore power effortlessly—designer suit, confident posture—yet Clara felt neither powerful nor confident. Only profoundly aware of how privilege, no matter who held it, came at someone else's expense.

The champagne flute in her hand suddenly felt too heavy. She thought of her father's gentle hands when he was her main caretaker while her mother traveling for work. She wondered what he'd think of this world. Of her place in it.

For the first time since arriving here, Clara acknowledged the uncomfortable truth: no matter which world you were in, justice tipped too far left scars. And now, she had to decide—would she be content benefiting from the imbalance, or would she dare to tip the scales?

The goosebumps on her arms had nothing to do with the air conditioning.

Clara couldn't resist the pull of curiosity. After hearing James' mentioning 'Dada for Dada', she found herself reaching for her phone, her fingers tapping quickly as she searched for the group. Within moments, she was scrolling through its website and social media pages, each one brimming with activity. The group's presence was everywhere—Facebook, Instagram, even niche forums where fathers shared their struggles, triumphs, and everything in between. Clara felt a strange mix of emotions as she began to dive into the world of these men, their stories unfolding before her like pages in a book she hadn't known she needed to read.

The first thing that struck her was the sheer honesty of the posts. These weren't polished, filtered snapshots of life; they were raw, unfiltered glimpses into the challenges of fatherhood in a society that often overlooked their contributions. One post, in particular, caught her eye. It was from a newly divorced single dad named Marcus, who had shared a photo of himself holding his toddler son in one arm while balancing a stack of bills in the other. His caption was simple but heartbreaking: "Trying to figure out how to make rent this month while still being there for my little boy. Any advice or resources would mean the world to us." The comments below were filled with encouragement, practical tips, and even offers of help from other dads who had been in his shoes. Clara felt a lump form in her throat as she read through them, her heart aching for Marcus and his son.

Another post was from a man named Daniel, who had recently become a full-time father after his wife's career took off. He wrote about the isolation he felt, the judgment he faced from others when his son had tantrums in public, and the pressure to prove he was still worthy of his wife's attention. "I love my kids more than anything," he wrote, "but some days, it feels like the world doesn't see me as anything more than a babysitter." The responses to his post were a mix of solidarity and advice, with many men sharing their own experiences of feeling invisible or undervalued. Clara found herself nodding along, her empathy growing with each word she read.

As she scrolled further, she came across a thread titled "Unexpected Heroes," where dads shared stories of small but meaningful victories. One man wrote about the first time he successfully braided his daughter's hair after weeks of practice, while another shared a photo of the elaborate dinosaur-shaped pancakes he had made for his son's birthday. These moments, though seemingly small, were clearly monumental to the men who shared them. Clara couldn't help but smile, her heart swelling with admiration for their dedication and love. They reminded her of those old days, when her dad baked cookies with her, with the sound of laughter echoing off sun-drenched walls, and the simple, profound joy of a cookie still warm from the oven.

But it wasn't all heartwarming stories. There were posts from dads struggling with postpartum depression, others grappling with the financial strain of single parenthood, and some who simply felt lost in their new roles. One man, named Javier, wrote about the guilt he felt for not being able to provide the kind of life he wanted for his children. "I work two jobs, but it's still not enough," he confessed. "I feel like I'm failing them every day". The outpouring of support in the comments was overwhelming, with dozens of men offering words of encouragement and sharing their own battles with similar feelings. Clara felt tears prick at the corners of her eyes as she read through the thread, her respect for these men deepening with every word.

By the time she set her phone down, Clara felt profoundly

moved. The world of 'Dada for Dada' was a testament to the strength, resilience, and love of these fathers—men who were navigating a society that often didn't see their worth. Their stories were a reminder that fatherhood, in all its forms, was a journey filled with both joy and hardship. As Clara sat there, reflecting on what she had read, memories of her own childhood began to surface, adding a deeply personal layer to her emotions.

She thought of her father, a kind and patient man who had always been there for her, especially when her mother's demanding work schedule kept her busy late into the evenings. Clara remembered how her dad would pick her up from school, help her with homework, and cook dinner with a calm efficiency that made it seem effortless. He was the one who taught her how to ride a bike, who stayed up late to comfort her after nightmares, and who never missed a school play or parent-teacher conference. Her father wasn't just a parent; he was a partner in every sense of the word, sharing the responsibilities of raising a family with her mother in a way that felt seamless and natural.

Clara's parents, both teachers, had always approached their roles as equals as possible. They split household duties, from cooking and cleaning to managing finances and planning family vacations. There was no such thing as "mom's job" or "dad's job" in their home—it was simply their job, a shared responsibility they tackled together as a team. Growing up in that environment had shaped Clara's understanding of what a family could be: a partnership built on mutual respect, collaboration, and love.

As she reflected on these memories, Clara felt a renewed sense of purpose. The men of Dada for Dada were living proof that fatherhood was not a lesser role but a vital one, deserving of recognition and support. They were doing the same work her father had done—work that had shaped her into the person she was today. These men deserved to be seen, to be celebrated, and to know that their efforts mattered. And if there was anything she could do to help, she was determined to do it. Whether it was through her business, her platform, or simply by lending an ear, Clara knew she had a role to play in creating a world where fathers like these felt valued and empowered.

With a quiet resolve, Clara thought to herself: she would use her voice and her influence to shine a light on the unsung heroes of fatherhood, just as her own father had been a hero to her. It was a small step, but one that felt deeply meaningful—a way to honor the lessons of her childhood and pay forward the love and support she had always known.

Clara phoned Ethan right away and told him that she decided to host a series of fundraising events specifically for *DADA for DADA*, using her established influence to raise both awareness and much-needed funds for the group's important work.

Although it started as a small gesture in the grand scheme of things, it was very welcomed and respected by the men involved. For them, Clara's decision to use her status to advocate for their cause felt like validation—an acknowledgment of the struggles they faced that so often went unrecognized. And for Clara, it was about more than just organizing events or raising money—it was about creating a space where empathy, understanding, and compassion could thrive.

As Clara stood in her gallery one evening during a fundraising event, surrounded by the art and the people she had come to know, she couldn't help but feel a sense of surrealism. Her life was a far cry from the one she had known, and yet, it felt strangely familiar. She had found success, but more importantly, she had found purpose.

She knew her journey was far from over. But for now, she was content. She had built a life that was not only successful but meaningful—a life that reflected her values, her empathy, and her unwavering belief in the power of art to change the world.

And as she looked out at the city skyline in dusk, she felt a quiet sense of gratitude.

CHAPTER 8: STRANGE PHONE CALL

Clara's fundraising events throughout NYC has been spread to many other major cities in the country. It has created a movement that raised a lot of attention in the female-dominated society.

Through her involvement, Clara was able to build a bridge between two worlds she knew well—her own experiences of fighting for recognition and respect in male-dominated spaces, and the overlooked yet equally powerful struggles of these fathers who were doing the vital work of raising children. She was keenly aware of how easy it could be to dismiss or minimize the challenges that men in these roles often faced. Yet, by opening up a platform for them to be heard, Clara hoped to create an environment where both men and women could come together to share, learn, and support each other.

One sunny September afternoon, Clara stood at the heart of the old Rockefeller Center, which has been called 'LindAI Plaza' after been bought by Linda 10 years ago, the vibrant energy of New York City pulsing around her. She gazed out at the diverse crowd gathered before her, their faces filled with curiosity and anticipation. With a confident smile, she stepped up to the microphone, her voice clear and resonant as she began to speak.

"Good afternoon, everyone. Thank you for being here today. I want to take a moment to talk about something that's close to my heart

—something that doesn't always get the attention it deserves. I'm here to talk about full-time dads. These are the men who wake before dawn to pack lunches with love, who spend their days soothing tears, helping with homework, and creating homes filled with warmth and security. They are the quiet architects of our future, shaping young minds with patience and devotion—and yet, too often, their contributions fade into the background of our daily lives.

In a world that sometimes overlooks the profound strength of modern fatherhood, we have the power—and the responsibility—to rewrite the story. These men aren't just 'helping out'—they're redefining what it means to nurture. Through their actions, they teach our children that love isn't gendered, that resilience is born in everyday moments, and that true strength lies in vulnerability. But this work shouldn't come at the cost of their wellbeing.

That's why I'm proud to announce new initiatives designed to honor their journey. Imagine parks, community centers, and malls with designated safe-zones—spaces where fathers can connect, breathe, and simply be, free from the pressures of our fast-paced world. Picture a first-of-its-kind social app where men find not just community, but professional guidance to navigate family struggles and physical challenges with confidence. Envision art and wellness centers designed just for them—with calming colors, ergonomic seating, and soothing soundscapes to ease the weight of their responsibilities. And for every dad balancing naptimes and household duties, we're expanding 'Dada for Dada' facilities to offer affordable yoga sessions, because self-care isn't selfish—it's sustainable leadership.

Let's be honest: society hasn't made this easy for them. Many face financial strain, isolation, or the quiet ache of feeling undervalued. But when we create spaces that acknowledge their struggles and celebrate their triumphs—when we truly listen to their stories without judgment—we don't just uplift fathers. We heal families. We strengthen communities. We prove that equality isn't about reversing roles, but about elevating every caregiver's dignity.

So today, I invite you to join this movement. Let's be the neighbors who offer to babysit so a dad can attend a support group. The employers who champion flexible schedules. The friends who say, 'You're doing an amazing job,' when the laundry piles up and the toddler won't nap. Because when we stand beside these men—when we honor their quiet revolutions at home—we don't just change their lives. We change what's possible for all of us.

Together, let's build a world where no father feels invisible, where every caregiver's labor is valued, and where the future is shaped by hands—both masculine and feminine—that hold each other up. Thank you."

As Clara stepped back from the microphone, leaving the stage to Linda who had been very supportive to all her public events. The crowd, filled with young families, erupted into applause, their cheers echoing through the plaza. She smiled, knowing that her words had struck a chord—and hopeful that they would inspire change, one family at a time.

Clara stepped back into her temporary meeting room on the 3rd floor of the LindAI Plaza, the hum of the city below fading as she closed the door behind her. The room was bathed in soft, natural light streaming through the floor-to-ceiling windows, offering a panoramic view of the bustling streets. She picked up the cappuccino Ethan had just made for her, its rich aroma filling the air as she took a long, satisfying sip. The warmth of the drink spread through her, and for a moment, she allowed herself to bask in a rare sense of self-satisfaction. She glanced out the window, watching the crowd below move like a living tapestry, and felt a quiet pride in how far she'd come.

But just as she was about to savor the moment, her phone rang, shattering the tranquility. The screen displayed an unfamiliar number; one she didn't recognize. Normally, Clara would have ignored it, dismissing it as spam or a wrong number. But today, feeling unusually lucky and generous, she decided to answer.

"Clara speaking," she said, her voice calm and professional.

There was no response—just silence on the other end. Clara waited a beat, her brow furrowing slightly. "Hello?" she tried again, but still, nothing. She hung up, a faint sense of unease creeping in. "Weird," she muttered to herself, setting the phone down on the table.

Before she could even process what had just happened, the phone rang again. This time, it was a different number. Clara hesitated, her fingers hovering over the screen. Something about this felt off, but curiosity got the better of her. She answered.

"Hello?" she said, her tone tinged with confusion.

"Good afternoon, Ms. Rose," came the reply. The voice on the other end was smooth and soothing, almost too polished. "My name is Skyler Johnson. I work for a tech company dedicated to the equalization of men and women. I'd like to show you our new AI cooking and cleaning products, which I believe could greatly benefit your upcoming fundraising event. May I have the honor of visiting your office tomorrow around 11 a.m.?"

Clara's initial unease softened slightly. The voice sounded young, polite, and earnest—likely a young man trying to make his way in the world. It wasn't uncommon these days for men, even those with prestigious degrees, to start their careers with cold calls like this. Still, something about the timing and the abruptness of the call felt… off.

"That sounds like a product with a good cause," Clara replied cautiously. "But I won't be in the office tomorrow morning. Could you confirm the schedule with my assistant first? Ethan can arrange it for you."

"Of course," the voice said smoothly. "Could you provide me with your assistant's phone number?"

Clara froze. Her instincts kicked in, and her voice sharpened. "How do you have my number but not my assistant's number?"

she asked, her tone now laced with suspicion.

Before she could get an answer, the line went dead. The abrupt "Beep Beep Beep" of the disconnected call echoed in her ears. Clara stared at her phone, her heart pounding. She felt violated, as if someone had intruded into her private space. The good mood she'd been enjoying just moments ago evaporated, replaced by a cold, unsettling feeling. "Who would do that?" she wondered aloud, her mind racing. "Is this some kind of prank?"

Pranks were rare in this world. People here were generally gentle and considerate, taught from a young age to regulate their emotions and avoid unnecessary conflict. Women were encouraged to manage their Firen carefully, while men were conditioned to be non-confrontational, almost as a survival mechanism. And with advanced AI cybersecurity systems in place, phone scams were practically unheard of. So why this? Why now?

Clara tried to shake off the unsettling feeling, but it clung to her like a shadow. She couldn't wrap her head around the strange call, but her busy schedule didn't allow her the luxury of dwelling on it for long. Just as she was about to refocus, Linda burst into the room, her energy electric and her face glowing with excitement.

"Darling!" Linda's voice brimming with enthusiasm. "Did you see the data? Your speech just hit over 3 million likes in the first two minutes! Every man in the world is going to be looking at you as their idol now!"

Clara stood there, stunned. The news should have filled her with pride, but instead, she felt a strange disconnect, as if the person they were celebrating wasn't really her. The weight of the strange phone call still lingered, casting a shadow over what should have been a triumphant moment. She managed a faint smile, but inside, her emotions were a tangled mess. It was as if she were watching someone else's life unfold—a life where 3 million likes and global admiration were the norm. But for Clara, it all felt surreal, almost too much to process.

"We've got to celebrate this with the other ROWFIRs at the Beekwomen Hotel tonight!" Linda exclaimed, her voice bursting with pride. Her eyes sparkled as she envisioned the evening—a gathering of powerful women toasting Clara's viral speech and its impact. "This is a moment worth celebrating, Clara. You've earned it!"

Clara forced a smile, nodding. "Of course," she replied, her voice warm but tinged with distraction. Her mind was still tangled with thoughts of the strange phone call earlier. The unsettling feeling lingered, but she didn't want to dampen Linda's spirits or burden her with something that might just be a minor blip in an otherwise perfect day. Tonight was about celebration, not confusion.

"Let's make it a night to remember," Clara added, her smile widening as she tried to match Linda's energy.

Linda clapped her hands, thrilled. "Perfect! I'll start making some calls."

Clara smiled back, though her mind drifted back to the phone call. A small part of her wondered: 'Who was on the other end of that call? And what did they want?' She couldn't shake the feeling that something wasn't right, but she pushed it down, determined to focus on the evening ahead. Tonight was about celebrating her achievements, surrounded by women who had become her allies and friends. Whatever the phone call meant, it could wait.

As Linda coordinated the evening, Clara glanced out the window, the city bathed in the golden hues of sunset. She imagined the night ahead—laughter, clinking glasses, and shared stories of triumph. It was a world she had worked hard to be part of.

The sharp trill of a phone pierced the air—Linda's secondary device, buzzing insistently from where it lay discarded on the antique side table. Clara turned, watching as Linda's fingers flew across the expansive foldable screen propped beside her, rescheduling meetings with the precision of a battlefield general. The ringing stopped, unnoticed.

Clara approached quietly. "Everything okay?"

Linda didn't look up. "Just clearing space for a finance group." Her stylus tapped rapidly, deleting one commitment, slotting in another. Then—a pause. She swiveled in her chair, fixing Clara with a gaze that held unexpected weight. "Why media?" she asked abruptly. "You never seem to take a breath."

The question hung between them. Linda exhaled slowly, as if steadying herself against a memory.

"My mother was an assistant director in the '90s," she began, her voice softer now. "I remember finding her once after a call, white-knuckling her desk, whispering, 'I'm so goddamn tired of taking orders from old white men who've never set foot on a set.'" A bitter smile. "Then the dot-com boom hit. She thought —finally—her chance. Started her own digital marketing firm. Poured everything into it."

Linda's fingers absently traced the edge of her screen. "VCs laughed her out of rooms. Literally. One told her to 'stick to making coffee.' So, she learned to play their game. Smiled at their jokes. Let them pat her shoulder. For twelve years." Her jaw tightened. "Then 2008 happened. Wiped her out. She filed for bankruptcy on a Thursday. Jumped from her office window on Friday."

A beat of silence. The hotel room's grand clock ticked loudly.

"I turned eighteen the day after her funeral," Linda continued, eerily calm. "Woke up here. In this world. Where the first investor who believed in me was a woman. Where my boardroom isn't a boys' club." She met Clara's eyes. "I don't get tired because I'm not surviving anymore. I'm living the life she should've had."

Clara reached out, squeezing Linda's hand. No platitudes. Just presence.

"Your mother would be proud," she said simply.

Linda's smile returned, lighter now. "Thank you." She stood, gathering her devices. "Now—Beekwomen at eight? Don't be late."

As the door clicked shut behind her, Clara stared at the vacant chair. The weight of Linda's confession settled over her—not as a burden, but as a reminder:

In this world, some women carried ghosts.

And sometimes, that was why they work so hard.

CHAPTER 9: SHADOWS IN THE NIGHT

The September evening was crisp and golden, the kind of night that wrapped the city in a cozy embrace. The air carried the faint scent of fallen leaves and the distant hum of New York City's relentless energy. The Beekwomen Hotel, recently upgraded with state-of-the-art AI security systems, stood as a beacon of modern luxury. Its sleek glass façade reflected the warm glow of the setting sun, while inside, the atmosphere was alive with the quiet hum of sophistication. Facial recognition scanners and voice identification technology now guarded every entrance, ensuring that only those with clearance could enter. It was a fortress of elegance, a sanctuary for the powerful women who gathered within its walls.

Clara stepped into the hotel's grand lobby, her heels clicking softly against the polished marble floor. The space was a masterpiece of design—low, ambient lighting, plush velvet seating, and art installations that seemed to pulse with life. She adjusted the strap of her clutch, her mind still lingering on the strange phone call from earlier. The unsettling feeling hadn't fully dissipated, but she pushed it aside, determined to enjoy the evening. Tonight was a celebration, after all.

As she made her way to the private lounge reserved for the ROWFIR gathering, she spotted Sarah and Nancy deep in conversation near the bar. Their voices were low, their tones intense, and their body language suggested they were discussing something serious. Clara approached them, her curiosity piqued.

"Clara, come over my dear" Sarah said, her sharp eyes locking onto hers. "We were just talking about the recent crime cases from BLAND. We shall all be alerted."

Nancy's expression grim. Sarah continued, "BLAND kids have been using scam calls to locate their targets. Once they have their location, they find a way to rob or even kill."

"That's terrifying." Nancy said with unease.

Clara's stomach dropped. The strange phone call from earlier suddenly felt far more sinister. "I had a weird call today," she admitted, her voice tense. "Two calls, actually. The first one was silent, and the second was from someone claiming to work for a tech company. They asked for my assistant's number, but when I questioned how they got mine, they hung up."

Sarah's eyes narrowed. "That's not a coincidence. Give me your phone."

Clara handed it over, her hands started to shake, and her heart pounding as Sarah examined it. The head of the NYPD was known for her sharp instincts and no-nonsense approach. Sarah flipped the phone over, her fingers probing the edges of the case. Suddenly, she paused, her expression darkening. "There's a tracer inside your phone cover," she said, her voice low and urgent. "They've been tracking you."

Clara felt a chill run down her spine. "What? How?"

"BLAND kids are getting smarter," Sarah muttered, her jaw tightening. She immediately pulled out her own phone and dialed a number. "This is Sarah Jones. I need you to trace two numbers immediately." She rattled off the details of Clara's strange calls, her tone leaving no room for argument.

Nancy, usually calm and composed, looked visibly shaken. "This just changed everything. If they're targeting Clara, they could be targeting all of us."

Sarah nodded and turned to Clara, "Sorry, Clara. No wine and cheese celebration tonight." her mind racing. She began dialing another number, but before she could connect, her phone rang. It was Emily.

"Sarah," Emily's voice was urgent, almost breathless. "You need to leave. Now. Evacuate the hotel. I can't reach the others, but my source just informed me that BLAND has a plan to storm the Beekwomen Hotel tonight."

Sarah's face went pale. "Understood. We're moving." She hung up and turned to Clara and Nancy. "We're leaving. Now."

Without waiting for a response, Sarah grabbed Clara's phone and smashed it against the edge of the bar, the screen shattering into pieces. "I will get you a new one with better security figures." she said grimly. She then went to open the door and pulled out her NYPD badge, issuing orders to the hotel staff, her voice commanding and authoritative. "Evacuate the building. Now. This is not a drill."

The calm lobby shattered. A tense voice crackled over the intercom, ordering an immediate evacuation. A frozen second of silence broke into a wave of pure fear. Well-dressed guests dropped their drinks, their polite chatter turning to sharp, frightened cries. People shoved past, scrambling for the doors as staff shouted directions, their faces tight with panic. Every second felt like a lifetime, every unknown shadow a potential threat, as the crowd surged toward the exits and the hope of safety. Sarah's grip was firm on Clara's elbow, propelling her and a trembling Nancy through a service door hidden in the paneling. Her other hand never left the textured grip of her Glock, still secured in its holster but screaming its silent promise of violence. The private elevator doors sighed open at her keycard's swipe. She herded them inside, her eyes constantly scanning the abandoned hallway. As the doors closed, sealing them in a tomb of brushed steel, she finally met their terrified stares. "We're going to NYPD headquarters," she said, her voice low and stripped of all comfort. "It's the only place they won't dare follow."

The ride down to the underground garage was tense, the silence broken only by the soft hum of the elevator. Clara's mind raced, her thoughts a jumble of fear and confusion. Who were these BLAND kids? Why were they targeting her? And what did they want from the ROWFIRs?

As they stepped into Sarah's armored SUV, Nancy broke the silence. "Do you think this is about us? Are they targeting the ROWFIRs specifically?"

Sarah's grip tightened on the steering wheel. "I don't know. But I think they're after something bigger, we need to be prepared. BLAND has been quiet over the decade. This could be the start of something much worse."

The drive to NYPD headquarters was a blur of flashing lights and distant sirens. Clara stared out the window, her mind replaying the events of the day. The strange calls, the tracer in her phone, the urgency in Emily's voice—it all felt like pieces of a puzzle she couldn't quite solve.

When they arrived, the NYPD building loomed before them—a formidable bastion of pale stone and gleaming dark glass, its facade etched with the names of heroes. The steps leading to the entrance were broad and flanked by two majestic stone lions, symbols of unwavering protection. Inside, the environment was a purposeful blend of authority and reassurance. The lobby was brightly lit and bustling with a diverse force of officers, a significant number of whom were capable-looking women who offered Clara and Nancy nods of calm, professional solidarity. Sarah wasted no time, cutting a direct path through the secure checkpoints. She escorted them past a heavy, bullet-resistant door and into a quiet, sanitized conference room where a focused team of officers, including a sharp-eyed female detective, was already waiting, case files spread across the table. "I want every available resource on this," she barked. "Trace those numbers, monitor activities from BLAND, and get me updates every fifteen minutes."

The officers nodded and sprang into action, their movements efficient and precise. Clara sat down, her legs feeling like jelly. Nancy placed a reassuring hand on her shoulder. "We'll figure this out," she said softly. "We always do."

But as the minutes ticked by, the updates were anything but reassuring. The numbers from Clara's strange calls were untraceable, ghost numbers that disappeared into the digital void. There was no news from the Beekwomen Hotel, no reports of an attack. It was as if the threat had vanished into thin air.

Just as the tension in the room reached its peak, Sarah's phone rang again. It was Emily. "They've dropped the plan," Emily said, her voice tinged with relief. "My source says BLAND has called off the attack. For now."

Sarah exhaled sharply, her shoulders relaxing slightly. "Any idea why?"

"Not yet. But my girls will keep digging." Emily responded.

As Sarah relayed the news to the room, Clara felt a mix of relief and unease. The immediate threat was over, but the questions remained. Why had they been targeted? And what did BLAND want?

Nancy leaned back in her chair, her expression thoughtful. "This feels like it's connected to ROWFIRs. Our identities may already be compromised."

Sarah's eyes narrowing, "I agree. And whatever it is, they're willing to go to extreme lengths to get it."

Clara didn't know what to make of it. She looked at the two women she admired very much. The evening was intended to be a celebration, but ended in chaos. Only one thing was clear to her at the moment: the world, she thought she had succeeded in, was far more dangerous than she had ever imagined. And as she sat there, surrounded by the hum of activity and the weight of unanswered questions, she had a strong instinct—this was only the beginning.

The NYPD headquarters was a fortress of steel and concrete, its sterile halls buzzing with the controlled chaos of officers and staff moving with purpose. Clara sat in the secure conference room, her hands trembling slightly as she clutched a bottle of water from a near table. The adrenaline that had carried her through the night was beginning to fade, leaving behind a hollow, gnawing fear. She stared at the table. Her mind went blank for a few minutes and then started replaying the events of the evening—the strange phone calls, the tracer in her phone, the frantic evacuation from the Beekwomen Hotel. It all felt surreal, like a nightmare she couldn't wake up from.

The door to the conference room swung open, and Clara looked up to see Linda and Evelyn stride in, their presence immediately filling the room. Linda's usually vibrant demeanor was subdued, her face pale but determined. Evelyn, ever composed, carried herself with the calm authority of someone who had faced crises before. Both women looked as though they had rushed here, their hair slightly disheveled and their coats thrown on haphazardly.

"Emily called us," Linda said, her voice tight with urgency. "She told us about the threat tonight. We came as soon as we could."

Evelyn went straight up to Clara and gave her a tight hug and a kiss on the head. Clara rested her head on Evelyn's arm a second.

Sarah, who had been pacing near the window, stopped and turned to face them. Her expression was a mix of relief and frustration. "Good. I'm glad to see you all safe and sound here." She gestured to one of her officers. "Take the ladies to the secure meeting room down the hall. I want detailed notes on anything suspicious they've noticed recently. No detail is too small."

The officer answered, "Yes, Ma'am." As they moved toward the door, Evelyn subtly pulled out her phone and typed a quick message. Clara felt Sarah's phone buzz near her. Sarah glanced at it and saw a text from Evelyn in a group chat with Nancy and Linda: "Don't talk about ROWFIR to anyone other cops except Sarah. Keep it between us."

Linda, standing nearby, noticed Clara looking at Sarah's phone. She leaned over and showed Clara her own screen, where the same message was displayed. Her eyes met Clara's, and for a moment, there was a silent understanding between them. To outsiders, they were just a group of lady friends who gathered for drinks and chats once a while. The true was: ROWFIRs were a tightly knit group, bound by trust and secrecy. Whatever was happening tonight, they needed to protect each other.

Clara nodded faintly, her throat too tight to speak. She felt paralyzed, her mind a whirlwind of fear and confusion. The weight of the evening pressed down on her, and she couldn't shake the feeling that she was still being watched, still being hunted. Her hands trembled as she set her coffee cup down, the liquid inside sloshing slightly. She wanted to say something, to ask questions, to voice her fears, but the words wouldn't come. It was as if her voice had been stolen, leaving her stranded in a sea of unspoken thoughts.

Linda noticed Clara's silence, her vibrant energy momentarily dimmed by concern. She stepped closer and placed a gentle hand on Clara's shoulder. The warmth of her touch was a small but grounding comfort. "Clara," she said softly, her voice filled with a tenderness that only someone who truly cared could muster. "How are you feeling?"

Clara looked up, her wide, haunted eyes meeting Linda's. She opened her mouth to respond, but the words caught in her throat, trapped by the weight of her fear. Instead, she shook her head slightly, her lips pressed into a thin, trembling line. The shock of the evening had left her feeling like a stranger in her own body, disconnected from the world around her. The once-cozy September night had turned into a nightmare, and Clara was struggling to find her footing.

Evelyn, ever observant and always composed, stepped closer. Her presence was like a steadying force, her calm demeanor cutting through the tension in the room. "She's in shock," Evelyn said to Linda, her tone firm but gentle. She reached out to the nearest couch and grabbed a blanket to wrap around Clara. "This will help. Give her a moment."

Linda nodded, though her worry was evident in the way her brow furrowed and her lips tightened. She went up to Clara and gave her a reassuring hug, her arms lingering for a moment longer before she followed the officer out of the room. As the door closed behind them, Clara was left alone with Sarah and a few other officers. The room, once bustling with activity, now felt colder, the silence heavy and oppressive.

Sarah, the head of the NYPD and a pillar of strength, walked over and sat down across from Clara. Her expression softened, the sharp edges of her usual no-nonsense demeanor giving way to something kinder, more maternal. "Clara," she said, her voice steady but infused with warmth. "I know this is a lot to process. You're safe here. We're going to figure this out."

Clara looked at her, her eyes searching Sarah's face for reassurance. She wanted to believe her, to trust that everything would be okay, but the fear was too deep, too raw. It clung to her like a shadow, refusing to let go. Sarah moved to sit next to Clara and placed her hand over Clara's, her touch firm and grounding. "We're here for you," Sarah said, her voice unwavering. "Whatever you need, we've got your back."

Clara's breath hitched, and for the first time since the chaos began, she felt a flicker of gratitude amidst the fear. It was a small spark of warmth in the cold, dark void that had taken hold of her. She took a deep breath, her chest rising and falling as she tried to steady herself. "What should I do now?" she asked, her voice trembling. "Are we waiting for something here? I don't feel safe anywhere else. I don't think I can go home. Where should I go? What if they want me dead? Do you think they know I'm here right now?"

Sarah's expression didn't waver. She pulled Clara into a firm, reassuring hug. When she pulled back, she looked directly into Clara's eyes, her gaze steady and unwavering. "You are safe here," she said, her voice leaving no room for doubt. "I will arrange a safe house for you until the situation is clear. No one is going to hurt you. Not on my watch."

Clara felt some of the tension leave her body, her shoulders relaxing slightly as she exhaled. "Thank you," she whispered, her voice barely audible. "I don't know what I'd do without you. Honestly, this all feels like a dream to me. It started as a peculiar but nice dream, and now it feels more like a nightmare."

Sarah smiled softly, her hand still resting on Clara's shoulder. "Darling, I've had those feelings too, especially with my job. But at least we've found each other, and we're here to help one another. No matter what this world throws at us, we'll face it together. We are ROWFIR. We don't back down, and we don't leave anyone behind."

A deep, shuddering sob broke from Clara's lips, the dam of her composure finally giving way. Sarah's heartfelt words settled in her soul. Hot tears traced paths down her cheeks, each one carrying away a fragment of the weight she had carried alone. And in that raw, vulnerable release, something unexpected happened—she didn't feel broken. She felt cleansed. The warmth of Sarah's unwavering belief seemed to seep into her, a steadying hand on her shaking heart. It was more than comfort; it was a transfer of strength. For the first time in what felt like forever, Clara felt the solid ground beneath her feet again, and rising in her chest was a fragile, but undeniable, glimmer of hope.

Seeing that Clara had calmed down, Sarah turned to her assistant, a strikingly handsome man with an air of quiet efficiency. "Prep some tea for the ladies," she instructed, her tone brisk but not unkind. As he moved to carry out her orders, Sarah began making calls to the political leaders in town—the mayor, the governor, and the senator, all powerful women who commanded respect and influence. Her voice was sharp and authoritative, each word carrying the weight of someone who knew how to get things done.

After the calls, Sarah turned back to Clara, who was now holding a steaming cup of tea, the warmth seeping into her hands. "Looks like there's no news from other sources," Sarah said, her tone thoughtful. "Let's go see Linda and Evelyn. I have something to discuss with everyone."

Sarah slipped a steadying arm around Clara's trembling shoulders, guiding her gently down the hall as if she could absorb her vulnerability with every step toward the secure room. It was a space designed for secrecy and safety, with explosive-proof walls, voice-proof insulation, and no windows. Beyond its walls, the room was a vault of perfect silence, invisible and impenetrable to the outside world. Yet within, it was a sanctuary. Soft light glowed upon a lush, fresh carpet, and vibrant bouquets bloomed in the corners, filling the air with a gentle rosy fragrance. It was a fortress within a fortress, but warm and inviting—a sacred space where the ROWFIRs could finally speak their truth, their words held in absolute confidence, forever sealed within its cozy embrace.

As they stepped inside, Clara felt a strange sense of calm. The room was a reminder that, no matter how chaotic the world outside became, she was surrounded by women who would fight for her, who would protect her, and who would never let her face the darkness alone. And in that moment, she knew she wasn't just a victim of circumstance—she was part of something bigger, something powerful. She was ROWFIR. And together, they would face whatever came next.

CHAPTER 10: A SHORT NOTICE

The meeting room was bathed in the soft glow of overhead lights, casting long shadows across the polished mahogany table. Despite the comforting scent of rose from an AI operated diffuser and air purifier, the air was inevitably thick with tension still. ROWFIRs sat around the table. Their faces etched with concern, determination, and a shared understanding of the gravity of the situation.

Sarah, the de facto leader of the group, stood at the head of the table, her sharp eyes scanning the room. Her presence was commanding, yet there was a warmth to her that made everyone feel seen and heard. She cleared her throat, drawing the attention of the room.

"Ladies" Sarah began, her voice steady but laced with urgency. "As you know, we're facing an unprecedented threat. Emily is also on her way, and she'll be here shortly." She paused, taking a deep breath. "One thing to mention first, I've just dispatched a police force to Clara's home, office building and the gallery. We're hoping to find any clues that might help us understand what we're up against. Clara, I know this is unsettling. We can't afford to wait."

Clara gave a slow, measured nod from her seat at the heart of the table. A fragile calm had settled over her features, belying the silent struggle still playing out in her lap, where her knuckles were white from the force of her clenched grip. She was a woman familiar with the sting of adversity, each past battle forging a resilience that had never failed her. But this… this felt less like a battle and more like a war, of a scale and depth she had never before encountered.

Before Sarah could continue, the door to the meeting room swung open, and Emily strode in. Her presence was electric, a force of nature that immediately shifted the energy in the room. She was dressed in a sleek, tailored suit, her hair pulled back into a no-nonsense ponytail. Her eyes, sharp and focused, scanned the room as she made her way to the table.

"Sorry I'm late," Emily said, her voice crisp and authoritative. "I've just received critical information from a military source. It's urgent, and it changes everything."

The room fell silent, all eyes on Emily. She placed a folder on the table and opened it, revealing a series of documents and photographs. "BLAND is on the move," she began, her tone grave. "They've shifted their focus to targeting female political leaders. This isn't just about intimidation—it's terrorism, plain and simple. And it's escalating."

She paused, letting the weight of her words sink in. "Our sources indicate that BLAND has recently upgraded their mini-nukes. They're more powerful, more precise, and they're ready to deploy. Their new targets? The personal residences of political figures. They're not just going after public spaces anymore—they're coming for homes, for families."

A collective gasp rippled through the room. The women exchanged worried glances, the reality of the threat hitting them like a tidal wave. Clara, however, remained silent, her brow furrowed in thought. Finally, she spoke, her voice steady but tinged with confusion.

"I'm not in politics," Clara said, her eyes locking with Emily's. "Why am I being targeted?"

Emily hesitated for a moment, her expression softening. "Clara, your work as an advocate for Dads' struggle and your influence in the community have made you a symbol of empowerment. Not sure why BLAND sees you as a threat, since you are not in any political position, but what you represent might be sensitive to them. If they want to silence you, they will send a message to you, as how they always do to people dare to challenge their agenda."

A cold, dread-heavy weight settled in Clara's chest, making it hard to breathe. She was never keen on the glaring lights of politics and public scrutiny. She just wanted to be a good person and do good things. Although, she had always known that her work came with risks. But this—this was beyond anything she had imagined. She glanced around the table, seeing the same fear reflected in the eyes of her sisters. But there was something else too—a fierce determination, a refusal to back down.

Sarah stepped forward, placing a reassuring hand on Clara's shoulder. "We're not going to let them win," she said, her voice firm. "We've faced challenges before, and we've always come out stronger. This time will be no different."

Emily nodded in agreement. "We need to act quickly. We'll increase security for all of you, especially at your homes. We'll also work with law enforcement to monitor BLAND's movements and gather as much intelligence as possible. But we need to be prepared for anything."

Clara found herself lingering behind, her mind racing with thoughts of what lay ahead. Sarah approached her, her expression a mix of concern and determination.

"Clara, I know this is a lot to process," Sarah said gently. "But you're not alone in this. We'll do whatever it takes to keep you safe."

Clara nodded, a small, grateful smile tugging at her lips. "Thank you, Sarah. I just… I never thought it would come to this."

"We can't always run away from them, when they determine to

come after us," Sarah replied. "We don't start a fight, but we will finish it."

Suddenly, Sarah's phone rang, slicing through the conversation like a knife. The sharp, insistent tone made everyone freeze mid-sentence. Sarah's eyes flicked to the screen, and her expression shifted instantly. Her usual calm demeanor hardened into something more serious, more focused. She held up a hand to silence the room, her gaze locked on the phone as she answered.

"Sarah speaking," she said, her voice clipped and professional. The room fell silent; every pair of eyes fixed on her. She listened intently, her brow furrowing as the person on the other end spoke. After a moment, she nodded sharply. "I hear you. Bring it to me."

She hung up and set the phone down on the table with deliberate precision. The sound of it hitting the wood seemed to echo in the sudden stillness. All eyes were on her now, waiting for an explanation. Sarah took a deep breath, her gaze sweeping the room before she spoke.

"We've got a package from BLAND," she said, her tone low and steady.

The words landed like a punch. Nancy, seated to Sarah's left, gasped audibly, her hand flying to her chest. "What do you mean?" she asked, her voice trembling with distress. "A package? From 'them'?"

Sarah nodded. Her expression grim. "The team I sent to Clara's office found a box on her desk. It had the BLAND logo on it. They scanned it for explosives or tracking devices, but there's nothing inside except a piece of paper."

Linda, always the most impatient of the group, leaned forward, her eyes narrowing. "What does it say?" she demanded, her voice sharp with urgency.

Sarah's lips pressed into a thin line. "You'll see for yourself in a moment," she said, her tone leaving no room for argument.

"Damn it, Sarah, just spit it out!" Linda snapped, her frustration boiling over. "We don't have time for your cryptic—"

Before she could finish, the room's AI voice interrupted, smooth and calm but impossible to ignore. "Package delivery has arrived. Requesting permission to open the door."

Sarah didn't hesitate. "Permission granted," she said, her voice firm.

The door slid open with a soft hiss, and a sleek, black police drone hovered into the room. It was a compact, high-tech machine, its propellers whirring quietly as it navigated the space with precision. Dangling beneath it was a small black box, unassuming but ominous. The drone glided to the center of the room, its sensors locking onto the table. With a mechanical whir, it released the box, which landed with a soft 'thud' in front of Sarah.

For a moment, no one moved. The box sat there, dark and foreboding, like a ticking time bomb. Sarah reached for it, her movements deliberate and unhurried. She lifted the lid, revealing a single sheet of paper inside. The women around the table leaned in, their breaths held, as Sarah unfolded the note and laid it flat on the table.

No envelope. No stamp. Just a single sheet.

The words glared up at her in jagged, uncompromising type:

UNITED BLAND

Beneath it, a message so simple it turned her blood to ice:

"Hello ROWFIRs. We want to talk."

The room went dead silent. The words seemed to hang in the air, heavy with implication. No one spoke for what felt like an eternity. Clara was the first to break the silence, leaning back in her chair with a dry, almost amused expression.

"Well," she said, her voice light but laced with irony, "looks like they don't want me dead yet."

Emily, ever the strategist, was already analyzing the message. "They know about us and they want something from us," she said, her tone thoughtful. "That's a first. They've never reached out like this before."

Linda, still visibly agitated, threw up her hands. "What could they possibly want? They're terrorists, for God's sake! Since when do they 'talk'?"

"We will have to wait for more information to figure that out. They have tracked down Clara. They could have eyes on all of us." Sarah sounded a bit disturbed.

Emily's eyes remained fixed on the note, her mind racing. "We won't know until we engage with them," she said finally, her voice steady but resolute. "This could be a trap, or it could be an opportunity. Either way, we need to find out what they're after."

Nancy, who had been quiet until now, spoke up, her voice trembling slightly. "But what if it's a trick? What if they're just trying to lure us into something?"

Sarah turned to her, her expression softening. "It's a risk," she admitted. "But if they're willing to communicate, it means they're feeling the pressure too. This could be our chance to turn the tables."

Clara crossed her arms, her gaze thoughtful. "Or it could be a distraction," she said. "Something to throw us off while they plan their next move."

Emily nodded in agreement. "Either way, we need to proceed carefully. We can't afford to underestimate them. We can't just wait for them to feed information to us. We need to take the initiative instead."

The room fell into a tense silence as the weight of the situation settled over them. The drone, having completed its task, hovered silently in the corner, its sensors still active, as if waiting for further instructions. The black box sat open on the table, the note inside a stark reminder of the danger they were facing.

Sarah straightened, her posture radiating determination. "How about set up a secure line of communication?" she suggested, her voice firm. "We'll hear them out, but on our terms. And we'll be ready for whatever they throw at us."

The women around the table exchanged glances, their expressions a mix of fear, resolve, and determination. They were a formidable group, each with her own strengths and vulnerabilities. But in that moment, they were united by a shared purpose: to protect each other, to stand up to the threat, and to fight for what they believed in.

Emily leaned forward, her elbows resting on the table, her sharp eyes scanning the room. She was the strategist, the one who always thought three steps ahead. Her voice was low, measured, and carried an air of authority that demanded attention.

"Sarah, you are right. Communication is needed. But we have to do it quietly. The world doesn't know about ROWFIRs yet. Here's what we can do," Emily began, her tone calm but firm. "Clara, you'll take the box back to your desk tomorrow morning. Hold it and walk through the 5th Ave before you go to your office. Act as if nothing happened and it just a box of donuts for office party. Go about your day like usual. BLAND is watching—we can be sure of that. If they see you returning the box to its original location, it'll intrigue them. They'll think we're ready for the next talk or lure them into a trap."

Clara's eye wide open. Her expression thoughtful. "And what about the box itself? Do we leave it empty?"

Emily's lips curled into a faint, almost imperceptible smile. "No. We leave them a message of our own."

The room seemed to freeze, time itself holding its breath as Emily leaned forward, her piercing gaze sweeping across the table. The air was electric, charged with the kind of tension that comes when the stakes are life and death. The black box from BLAND sat ominously in the center of the table, its presence a silent reminder of the danger they were in. Emily's voice cut through the silence, low and deliberate, as she laid out the plan.

"This is how we turn the tables," she began, her tone sharp and unyielding. "It's bold. It's risky. But it's the only way to keep BLAND guessing." She paused, letting the weight of her words sink in. "We're not just responding—we're countering. And we're going to make them think they've won… right up until the moment they realize they've walked into our trap."

The women exchanged glances, their faces a mosaic of apprehension, determination, and quiet resolve. This wasn't just a plan—it was a high-stakes gamble, a chess moves in a game where the consequences of losing were unthinkable.

Emily reached for a blank sheet of paper and a pen, her movements slow and deliberate, as if every second carried the weight of the world. She wrote a single sentence in clear, bold letters:

"Clara will meet you at Central Park at midnight tomorrow."

She held up the note, her expression unreadable, her eyes locked on the group. "This is our message," she said, her voice steady but laced with intensity. "BLAND may be watching us for awhile. If BLAND finds this message, they'll understand they've got our attention. Or believe Clara is walking into their scheme. By making direct contact, we'll be watching every move they make and figuring out what they know about us and what they want."

Clara, who had been silent until now, leaned back in her chair, her arms crossed. Her face was calm, but there was a flicker of tension in her eyes, a quiet storm brewing beneath the surface. "You're using me as bait," she said, her voice steady. It wasn't a question.

Emily met her gaze without flinching, her expression hard and unyielding. "Yes," she said bluntly. "But not in the way they'll expect. We'll have eyes on the park long before they arrive. Surveillance, snipers, undercover agents—we'll control the entire area. If they show up, we'll be ready. And if they don't… well, we'll have learned something valuable about their attitude.

The room fell silent, the weight of the plan settling over them like a heavy fog. It was a gamble, a dangerous one, but it was also their best shot at gaining the upper hand. Everyone nodded slowly. Clara's expression resolute. "Alright," she said, her voice firm. "Let's do it."

The next phase of the plan unfolded with military precision, Emily's sharp mind guiding every detail. She turned to Clara, her tone clipped and authoritative. "You'll return the box to your desk first thing in the morning. Make sure you're seen—but don't draw attention to yourself. Act natural. If BLAND is watching, they'll assume you're aware of their message. And they will be intrigued by what's your next move."

Clara nodded, her mind already racing through the logistics. "What if they try to intercept me before I get to the office?" she asked, her voice calm but edged with concern.

"We'll have a security detail on you at all times," Emily replied without hesitation. "Discreet, but close enough to intervene if needed. You won't be alone."

Emily's gaze shifted to the rest of the group, her voice dropping to a near whisper. "After you place the box, Clara, you'll leave your office and instruct your assistant that no one is allowed to enter. BLAND will find their own way in—maybe even under our watch. And when they do, we'll be ready."

She turned back to Clara, her expression grim. "You'll need to prepare for the meeting. We'll outfit you with a wire and a tracking device. If things go south, we'll know exactly where you are and how to extract you."

Clara raised an eyebrow, her tone dry. "You think it'll come to that?"

Emily's jaw tightened. "I hope not," she said, her voice low. "But we need to be ready for anything."

Sarah stepped in, her voice calm but commanding. "I can arrange my team to coordinate the surveillance operation. We'll need eyes on every entrance to the park—cameras, drones, undercover agents. We will have complete coverage. If BLAND shows up, we'll know before they even step foot in the park."

Emily nodded, a faint smile playing on her lips. "Exactly."

But then Nancy, who had been quietly observing, leaned forward, her brow furrowed. "One question, though," she said, her voice tinged with concern. "How are we going to keep hiding our ROWFIR identity if your police force is going to be overhearing the talk between BLAND and us? If they find out who we are, this whole operation could blow up in our faces."

Emily's warm smile dissolved into something far more formidable. Her piercing gaze swept across the circle of curious faces. Her laughter lines and silver streaks spoke of hard-won wisdom. Leaning forward, she lowered her voice to a conspiratorial murmur that made every woman instinctively draw closer. "Here's where it gets interesting," Emily confided, her voice rich with the confidence of someone who had navigated decades of bureaucratic battles. "I will issue a secretive spy training order, coded 'ROWFIR', making it a classified spy training protocol that exists in only one file, accessible solely by me. Her manicured finger tapped the table for emphasis. "And we have an ace in the hole: the Navy's 'Buffalo Unit'—an all-female special ops team specializing in invisible warfare. No leaks, no slip-ups. This operation stays airtight." Her gaze swept the room, landing on each woman for a brief moment, as if silently reinforcing the gravity of what they were about to undertake.

Sarah, ever the pragmatist, raised an elegant eyebrow. "And the police?"

Emily's lips curved knowingly. "Oh, NYPD will have their role—keeping streets secure, none the wiser that we're running the real operation. We'll feed your police force just enough to keep them content. No offense, Sarah."

"None taken." Sarah waved her hand.

Both of their tones carried the patient amusement of a mother humoring children, a skill every woman in the room recognized from their own lives.

Emily's fingers dipped into her front pocket with deliberate grace, retrieving an object so small it could have been mistaken for a button from a well-tailored blazer. But as she held it up between her thumb and forefinger, the overhead lights caught the sleek, matte-black surface of the device—no larger than a dime, yet humming with quiet power.

"This," she said, her voice dropping to a hush thick with meaning, "is Clara's lifeline."

"Meet 'Wind Whisper'," she murmured, turning the device so it caught the light. "Designed by the Buffalo Unit. It applies encrypted high frequency signals with AI adjustment according to the user's environment. It doesn't just transmit—it breathes. Crystal clear up to five meters, then…" She danced her fingers in air. "Gone. Dissolved into white noise. Not even the NSA's labyrinth of algorithms could trace it back to us." The pride in her voice was palpable—this was women's ingenuity at its finest.

"No one outside this room will know what's truly said in that meeting," Emily continued, her voice steel wrapped in velvet. "Not the NYPD. Not the public. Not the ghosts in the walls. This? This is ours."

Sarah's brow furrowed, her sharp mind already dissecting the risks. "The Buffalo Unit," she said slowly. "How do we know they won't talk?"

Emily didn't blink. "Because they're not just soldiers." Her voice softened, just slightly, as if stepping into a memory. "They're daughters of the First Nations. Granddaughters of women who survived hardships the history books never named. They are now Tech savants who built systems from scraps when the world gave them a chance for new life without ties to men. The Buffalo Unit doesn't just follow orders—they choose loyalty. And they chose me."

A silence fell, thick with the weight of trust and the ghosts of battles fought long before this one. The kind of silence that comes when everyone is holding their breath, absorbing the enormity of the plan.

"I like the sound of it." Nancy broke the silence.

"I felt that I heard of this unit before. Buffalo. Why it sounds so familiar?" Linda tried to recall.

"I know. It's the unit that set up the voice shield for our secret meeting room at Beekwomen Hotel before." Evelyn added.

A ripple of recognition passed through the group. Nancy's eyes lit up. "That formidable indigenous woman with the scar? The one who—"

"—could stare down a grizzly bear?" Evelyn finished with a chuckle.

"Yes, she is a special agent sent by me to supervise the hotel team for our safety." Emily revealed, "the buffalo unit is mostly filled with first nations women who turns out to be the most fearless and smart people in the navy. Ever since the discover of power from Firen, women in the aboriginal communities almost killed every male on their land. Many of them fought atrociously on battles against BLAND decades ago. Same as many women from previous black communities who are now very established in the air-force."

Clara's fingers traced the edge of the table, her throat tight. "It sounds… vengeful," she whispered.

Evelyn's sigh was the sound of a woman who had carried history in her bones for too long. "Oh, darling. It was." Her gaze drifted, as if staring through the walls into a past stained with blood and smoke. "Globally, whole male population almost erased. Some men escaped to BLAND with nothing but fear. Now they're

BLAND's sharpest weapons."

The conversation turned sober as they discussed history. Clara, ever the empath, voiced: "That's very destructional."

Evelyn turned to Clara, her wise eyes clouding. "Fear breeds rage, darling. It always has."

The hushed room was thick with unspoken thoughts. Each woman lost in her own private reverie. The soft glow of antique lamps around each corner, casting a pale light over their tired but alert faces. Though none had slept, exhaustion was the last thing any of them felt.

Then, at exactly 7 a.m., the smooth, disembodied voice of an AI speaker cut through the silence, its tone unnervingly cheerful. "Good morning, Madam! It's a new day to make history."

A few of the women exchanged glances—some amused, some weary, all knowing. They had been here before, caught in that strange limbo between night and morning, between fatigue and exhilaration. Was it the thrill of the hunt? The comfort of shared solitude? Or simply the quiet understanding that, at this hour, the world belonged to them—women who had seen decades of life, love, and loss, ready for whatever came next?

No one spoke. But in that charged silence, there was a silent agreement: "This is our time."

The next hour, Clara arrived at her office building as usual, the black box tucked securely under her arm. She moved with purpose but without haste, her expression calm and composed. As she entered the building, she made a point of greeting the security guard and exchanging a few words with a colleague in the elevator. If BLAND was watching, they would see nothing out of the ordinary.

She entered her office and placed the unmarked box precisely in the center of her polished desk. A single corner of Emily's note peeked out from under the lid, a deliberate flaw in an otherwise perfect scene. With meticulous care, she adjusted a pen, aligned a stack of files, and breathed on the surface to erase a faint smudge—returning everything to the exact state she'd left it in. For ten agonizingly normal minutes, the soft click of her laptop keys was the only sound. Then, rising, she informed her secretary with an air of unshakeable finality that her office was not to be entered under any circumstances, and that she would be… unavailable for the remainder of the day.

The box sat there, innocuous and unassuming. If BLAND showed up, they would walk into a trap of their own making. If they didn't, ROWFIRs would still have gained valuable insight into their tactics.

While a safe house was still getting ready under Sarah's order, the converted NYPD secure room had become a war room. And its current battle was against exhaustion and dread. In shifts, the ROWFIRs succumbed to fitful sleep, curled on chairs or against one another for comfort, their rest a temporary loan from the woman who never looked away. Sarah was their shield. Every ounce of her being was focused on the grainy video feed, her love for Clara sharpening her focus into a razor's edge. The world outside the monitors ceased to exist. Minutes bled into hours, the unchanging image of an empty office becoming a form of torture. The silence was a heavy blanket, smothering and ominous, and Sarah, with jaw clenched and eyes burning, dared it to break.

Finally, just after noon, the feed showed a figure entering Clara's office—a maintenance worker, or so it seemed. He moved quickly. His actions deliberate. He opened the box, removed the note, and slipped it into his pocket before leaving as quietly as he had come.

Emily leaned back in her chair, a satisfied smile playing on her lips. "They took the bait," she said. "Now we wait."

CHAPTER 11: AN INVITATION

Clara stood in front of her bedroom mirror, adjusting the vintage watch on her wrist—her father's last gift to her before the accident. The leather strap was worn soft with age; the face slightly scratched from years of use. She traced the edges with her thumb, as if she could summon his presence through the familiar weight of it. Beside it, she fastened her mother's pearl necklace, the cool beads settling against her collarbone like a whispered promise.

'Armor,' she thought.

She dressed carefully—a tailored black suit, a deep red blouse the color of old wine, freshly polished nails in a matching shade. Her shoes, handmade Italian leather, were both elegant and practical, designed for women who knew the difference between 'looking' powerful and 'being' powerful.

Outside, the armored NYPD van idled at the curb, its darkened windows hiding Sarah in the back seat. Clara took a steadying breath and stepped into the night, flanked by silent, stone-faced female officers.

The van's interior was tomb-silent—no rumble of an engine, just the occasional 'ping' of the electric dashboard coming to life. Clara had forgotten how unnerving these new vehicles could be, gliding through the city like ghosts. The absence of sound made everything feel sharper—the leather seat creaking under her, the whisper of Sarah's blazer as she shifted, the faint scent of gun oil and jasmine hand cream clinging to the NYPD chief's skin.

Then—warmth.

Sarah's hand closed over Clara's icy fingers without preamble; her grip calloused from years of holding a service weapon yet unexpectedly tender.

"Here is your new phone. We've got your back." Sarah's voice was low; the kind of tone women use in hospital hallways and courtrooms. "I'm proud of you."

Clara's throat tightened. Three years ago, she'd woken up in this strange world with nothing but her own fractured memories. Now? These women had become the family she'd lost—fierce, loyal, and unshakable. The kind who'd storm hell itself if one of their own was trapped inside.

The van moved through the city like a silent witness, its hybrid engine purring beneath them as lights passed in blurred streaks across the windows. Clara sat in the hush of the backseat, listening to the muted world outside, until finally—almost without realizing—she asked the question that had been pressing against her ribs for days.

"Sarah… why did you want to become a cop?"

There was a pause. Sarah didn't answer right away. She looked into Clara's eyes like she was verifying her identity. And then, she turned her head toward the window, her face cast in the shifting amber of the passing streetlights. For a moment, her expression was unreadable—carved from quiet stone.

Softly, her voice broke the silence. It was low and even, like someone lifting something heavy from a deep place.

"I was twenty," she said. "Working nights at a bar near the financial district. The kind of place with sleek marble counters and overpriced whiskey—the kind that looked respectable, but everyone inside wore their power like perfume. Expensive. Pungent. And suffocating."

She let out a small, humorless breath.

"Most of the staff were women. We had this unspoken code—signals, little gestures. If one of us got cornered by a customer who thought his black card entitled him to more than drinks, another would step in, distract him, steer him away. We were each other's shield. You had to be."

Her voice grew tighter, tinged with something darker.

"One night, a man reached for me. Bold, drunk, not bothering with pretense. His hand—" she faltered briefly, "—he touched me. Like I was on a menu. And then he laughed. Invited me to drink with his buddies, like nothing had happened."

Clara felt her own breath catch.

"My colleague saw it. Didn't even flinch. She slid in between us, started gushing about some new Cuban rum shipment, got their attention onto liquor and deals. I was shaken, but I stayed. I had to. That's when I realized—they weren't just drinking. They were negotiating something—money moving overseas, fake invoices, all in code. A few minutes later, she came back."

Sarah's eyes narrowed slightly, as if reliving every detail.

"She pulled out a badge. A real one. Officer Tan. Undercover. Within seconds, half a dozen plainclothes cops stood up, calm as shadows, surrounding the hot-headed guy. Clean sweep."

She paused, her lips twitching with something like awe.

"It was the first time I saw a woman hold that kind of authority. Not with a gun. With presence. With control. She didn't yell. She didn't posture. She just *was*. I admired her more than I knew how to say."

But the story didn't end in triumph.

Sarah's voice dropped again, brittle now.

"Two months later, I saw her obituary on the local newspaper. Officer Tan. Raped and chocked to death on her walk home. No suspects. But everyone whispered the same thing—it was retaliation. Gang-related. She died alone on a cold street."

The van grew still. Even the city's heartbeat outside seemed to hush.

"I couldn't go back to work. Couldn't sleep. Her face just wouldn't leave me. I kept seeing her hands, steady as she held that badge. And I kept wondering… if she knew what might come. And did it anyway."

Sarah stared at her own lap; her hands tightly knotted together like rope.

"Then one morning, I woke up here. In *this* world. No warning. No reason. Just… here. And I remembered her. Not just how she died—but how she *lived*."

She turned to Clara, her gaze clear now. Fierce. Unapologetic.

"I didn't hesitate. I knew what I had to do. This time, I wouldn't just admire strength from the sidelines. I'd become it."

The silence that followed didn't need words. Because in that moment, Clara understood: Sarah hadn't just chosen to wear the badge. She had chosen to carry a legacy. And perhaps, in this strange world of second chances, that was the most powerful thing of all.

The van had gone quiet after that, the city lights slipping across their faces like ghosts.

The van door slid open with a harsh, metallic shriek, a sound swallowed too quickly by the thick, damp air of the Manhattan night. Seventy-Second and Fifth.

Across the street, Central Park wasn't just a park; it was a living, breathing entity of darkness, a wall of impenetrable black that seemed to swallow the light whole. The amber glow of the streetlights didn't so much illuminate the path as it did cast long, twisted, and grasping shadows that bled across the asphalt. They were too long, too deep, moving with a life of their own just at the edge of her vision.

The flat, rubber soles of her shoes met the wet pavement with a soft, percussive thud, a muffled sound that was instantly suffocated by the dense air. It was the sound of a secret being kept, a stark contrast to the sharp, dry rustle as she shuffled through the carpets of fallen leaves., a frantic metronome counting down the seconds. She could feel the vibration travel up through the delicate bones of her feet, a sharp, staccato rhythm that matched the frantic, trapped-bird flutter of her heart. Her mind wasn't just blank; it was a vacuum, a screaming void where every normal thought had been violently scoured away by a cocktail of pure adrenaline and cold, clawing terror. They didn't cancel each other out; they were locked in a silent, screaming battle inside her, holding her body hostage, making every breath a conscious, shuddering effort.

The world around her wasn't just still—it was *waiting*. The air itself felt heavy and watchful, pressing against her skin like a cold, damp hand. The skeletal branches of the trees across the street were frozen in a grotesque dance, holding their breath. The entire city, for one heart-stopping moment, had paused. And in that profound, deadly stillness, Clara knew, with a certainty that iced her veins, that she was not alone.

Then— movement.

A figure detached itself from the darkness near the park's stone wall.

Clara's breath seized in her chest.

"Ethan."

He stood directly in her path, close enough that she could see the flecks of gold in his brown eyes—eyes she'd once trusted. The boyish smile he'd worn while bringing her coffee, while joking about his cousin's baby, while helping her hang artwork in the gallery—gone. Replaced by a calm so absolute it was more terrifying than any weapon.

"Hello, Clara."

Her pulse roared in her ears. This wasn't just betrayal. This was 'violation'. Every shared confidence, every moment of camaraderie—all calculated.

And the worst part?

Somewhere beneath the rage clawing up her throat, she still 'missed' the Ethan she'd thought she knew.

The park's wrought-iron gates creaked in the wind behind him like a warning.

Or an invitation.

"You?" Clara said with confusion.

Ethan didn't flinch. "BLAND appreciates what you've done for fathers," he said, as if they were discussing a business proposal. "We want you with us."

Clara's nails dug into her palms. "Was any of it real?"

"The mission was to approach you," he admitted. "But the respect? That wasn't pretend."

He pulled out a tablet casting a 3D hologram of operation space, swiping to a video—women draped in gold, seated like statues in a sunlit temple. "Goddesses," Ethan explained. "Worshipped, protected. BLAND isn't what you think. The leadership has changed. We don't want war."

Clara stared. The women in the footage were serene, untouchable. But something about their stillness unnerved her.

"You can have a career there," Ethan keeps swiping. "Art, influence—whatever you want. All ROWFIRs would be welcome."

Clara's mind raced. This wasn't the BLAND she'd been warned about—the violent, woman-hating fringe. This was... something else.

"I'm not here looking for new jobs," she said finally.

Ethan nodded. "Sleep on it. I'll take you there myself when you're ready. And if you hate it? I'll bring you back."

"Thanks for showing up tonight. Good night, Ethan." Clara did not like staying any longer.

The words "Good night, Ethan" tasted bitter on Clara's tongue as she turned away, leaving him swallowed by the shadows of Central Park. Her chest ached with a confusing tangle of emotions—betrayal, yes, but also an unexpected pang of loss for the friendship she'd thought was real. The frigid night air, sharp and biting as shattered glass, clawed at her lungs with each ragged breath, doing nothing to cut through the thick, syrupy fog of despair clouding her mind. Every step back toward the empty, mocking curb where she'd been left behind was a heavy, reluctant trudge, the journey feeling infinitely longer and more isolating than before, as if the very pavement were stretching out to prolong her anguish.

The van door slid open with a quiet hiss, revealing Sarah's concerned face illuminated by the soft blue glow of dashboard screens. Without a word, the police chief reached out and pulled Clara inside, her strong hands guiding her onto the plush leather seat.

"You're in shock," Sarah observed, her sharp eyes missing nothing as she took in Clara's pale complexion and trembling fingers. She wrapped a steadying arm around Clara's shoulders, the warmth of her touch cutting through the numbness. "I'm here. Whatever comes next, ROWFIRs walk through it together."

Clara let out a shaky breath, leaning into Sarah's solid presence. Three years ago, she'd been utterly alone in this strange world. Now, she had sisters who would stand between her and the storm.

"Where are we going?" Clara asked, her voice barely above a whisper.

Sarah's mouth curved into a tight but reassuring smile. "Somewhere safe. I've arranged a new safe house just for

ROWFIR—state-of-the-art security, untraceable." She squeezed Clara's hand. "We'll figure this out."

The safe house was nothing like Clara expected. Nestled in an unassuming Upper East Side brownstone, the interior had been transformed into a futuristic command center that would make any tech billionaire jealous.

Floor-to-ceiling smart glass windows could opaque with a voice command. The walls were embedded with advanced surveillance tech that monitored every approach. A holographic display dominated the central meeting space, currently projecting real-time data streams from across the city.

But what struck Clara most was the 'warmth' of the space—the plush sofas arranged in a cozy circle, the shelves lined with well-loved books, the kitchen stocked with premium coffee and wine. This wasn't just a bunker. It was a 'home'—one built by women who understood the need for both cutting-edge security and soft places to land.

The other ROWFIRs were already gathered around an antique oak table that somehow looked perfectly at home amidst the technology. Evelyn sat ramrod straight in her signature tailored suit, her sharp gaze fixed on a tablet. Nancy leaned forward, her silk blouse whispering as she traced a finger over a digital map. Linda paced behind them, a glass of red wine in hand, her designer indoor slippery sinking into the thick carpet. 'Nothing says "profoundly stressful time" like ensuring the throw pillows are fluffed and the artisanal sparkling water is properly chilled,' Clara felt ironic, watching the scene of serene, Instagram-ready luxury. The apocalypse could wait; there was a charcuterie board to assemble.

Emily looked up as Clara entered, her military-sharp posture softening just slightly. "There she is," she said, pushing a steaming mug of chamomile tea across the table. "Drink. Then we talk."

Clara wrapped her hands around the warm mug, letting the

floral scent soothe her frayed nerves as she sank into an embrace of soft leather. For the first time since Ethan's revelation, she felt her pulse begin to steady.

Sarah took her place at the head of the table, tapping a command into the holographic interface. Footage of Ethan's meeting with Clara appeared in the air above them, his words about BLAND's "goddesses" echoing through the room.

"Let's dissect this piece by piece," Sarah said, her voice calm but edged with steel. "Starting with the biggest question: those 'goddesses'—how are they not using Firen? Are there more ROWFIRs in BLAND like us?"

Around the table, the most powerful women in New York leaned in, their collective intelligence and experience forming an impenetrable shield around their youngest sister.

Clara took a slow sip of her tea, feeling its warmth bloom in her chest and ease the tight knot of fear in her stomach. A quiet sigh escaped her. Whatever storm was coming, she wouldn't have to face it alone. The thought of her ROWFIR sisters watching over her just felt like coming home to her parents' unconditional protection. In that moment, she was content to surrender her burdens, to be the one who was cared for instead of the one who had to figure out all the answers.

Linda pacing, "And how did BLAND hide this from our satellites?" She turned to Emily, as if the Navy would know more about it.

"Advanced shielding tech," Emily said grimly. "We've underestimated them."

Clara sat silent, her father's watch ticking softly on her wrist.

She had come to this world by accident. And her next move just became even more unpredictable.

The voices of the other ROWFIRs faded into a comfortable hum as Clara's eyelids grew heavy. Let the foreign affairs experts handle the situation—that was their world, not hers.

Drifting toward sleep, she found herself longing for the quiet anonymity of a simple life, a thought that carried her gently into unconsciousness.

She never heard the details discussed in the safehouse that night. Later, she would only vaguely recall Sarah's calm declaration that no further threats had been detected. By morning, she was back home, where new security systems—already seamlessly installed by Emily's Navy specialists—stood watch without a sound.

CHAPTER 12: A BUSINESS TRIP

Clara awoke to golden sunlight spilling across her bedsheets, the kind of morning that felt like a fresh start. For the first time in weeks, she didn't reach for her phone to check for threats or messages from ROWFIR. Instead, she lay still, breathing in the quiet—the distant chirp of sparrows, the hum of a lawnmower somewhere down the street. It reminded her of that very first morning in this world, when she'd opened her eyes to the impossible: a reality where women led, where power had a different shape. Back then, she'd been shocked. Today, she felt something else—a thrilling undercurrent of possibility.

The air was perfection itself as she stepped outside—crisp enough to invigorate but warm enough to go without a jacket. A gentle breeze carried the green, earthy scent of freshly cut grass, mingling with the faint sweetness of blooming hydrangeas from her neighbor's garden. Clara paused on her porch, eyes closed, just feeling it. Balanced. Peaceful. Like the universe itself had taken a steadying breath.

Her neighborhood in the New Jersey suburbs was alive with the soft rhythm of a weekday morning. Down the street, a group of fathers pushed strollers along the sidewalk, their laughter carrying on the breeze. Clara's gaze drifted toward the community park, where the newly installed "Men's Social Safe-Zone" buzzed with quiet activity. Under a canopy of oak trees, clusters of men sat at picnic tables, some sipping coffee while others leaned in for earnest conversation. A few snapped selfies—grinning, arms slung around each other's shoulders—undoubtedly to post later on GentleSpace, the male-friendly social app her foundation had helped launch. It was more than a platform; it was a lifeline, offering everything from parenting advice to confidential counseling for those struggling in their roles.

She walked on, her stylish yet practical loafers barely making a sound on the paved path. The "Art and Wellness Center"—one of her proudest projects—stood just beyond the park, its floor-to-ceiling windows glowing in the morning light. Inside, a dozen full-time dads moved through a sunrise yoga class, their mats arranged in neat rows. Some were clearly beginners, their movements tentative but determined. Others flowed through the poses with the ease of longtime practitioners. Near the front, a man in his fifties balanced effortlessly in tree pose, his toddler giggling from a supervised play area just off the mat.

Clara lingered in the doorway, unnoticed. The room itself was designed for tranquility—walls painted in soft, muted blues, ergonomic seating in warm walnut tones, and a sound system emitting a low, soothing frequency meant to ease stress. A far cry from the sterile gyms of her old world, where men were expected to "tough it out" on weight machines. 'This' was sanctuary.

One of the male instructors—a former voice actor/fulltime dad turned yoga teacher—caught her eye and smiled. Clara returned it, her chest swelling with quiet pride. This was why she'd fought so hard for these spaces. Not out of pity, but because she'd seen firsthand how stress could erode even the strongest spirits.

As she turned to leave, her phone buzzed. A notification from the 'Dada for Dada' network popped up: "8:30 AM Dad's Breakfast Club forming at Main St. Café. All welcome."

Clara exhaled, her breath stirring a loose curl at her temple. The world wasn't perfect. But it was 'progress'. And for now, that was enough.

Clara strode through the glass doors of her art foundation's exhibition center, the morning sun casting long, confident shadows behind her. The lobby hummed with quiet efficiency—staffs balancing tablets and coffee cups, curators debating frame selections in hushed tones near the modern sculpture display.

Then she saw him.

James stood behind the sleek marble reception desk; his broad shoulders slightly hunched over a shipping manifest. The morning light caught the silver strands at his temples—new since his daughter's birth. When he looked up and met Clara's gaze, his tired eyes crinkled into a warm smile.

"Good morning, Ms. Rose." His voice carried the quiet dignity of a man who took pride in his work, no matter how ordinary the task.

Clara paused, returning the smile with genuine warmth. "James. How's that beautiful baby girl of yours?"

His entire face transformed. "Sleeping through the night, finally." He chuckled, rubbing the back of his neck. "Though now my wife's talking about trying for another, since she her body is not getting younger."

The normalcy of the moment almost made Clara forget—until James leaned slightly forward, his expression shifting.

"Actually…I've been trying to reach Ethan for two weeks about the shipments for the new LA location. His voicemail's full." A faint line appeared between his brows. "That's not like him."

Clara's stomach tightened. The memory flashed—Ethan standing in Central Park's shadows, his boyish charm replaced by cold calculation. The Buffalo Unit's silent surveillance van parked outside his apartment since then, monitoring every move.

She kept her voice smooth as poured coffee. "He's on an unexpected business trip. Spotty service." A practiced lie, delivered with just the right mix of nonchalance and authority.

"If it's urgent, I can have Lydia assist you."

James studied her for half a second too long. Clara could almost see the questions forming—Ethan hadn't mentioned any trip; the gallery reopening was in ten days—but years of navigating workplace hierarchies kept him from voicing them.

"Nothing critical," he said finally, tapping the paperwork. "Just delayed canvases from Berlin and the lease renewal for the Chelsea space." He hesitated. "But if you hear from him…?"

"Of course." Clara's smile didn't reach her eyes. "I'll have Lydia email you the shipping updates by noon."

As she turned toward the elevator, her professional flat heels clicking with deliberate confidence, Clara felt the weight of the unspoken pressing against her ribs. James was no fool. He'd known Ethan for years—had shared beers after late nights preparing exhibitions, had covered his shifts when his daughter was born.

The elevator doors slid shut. Clara exhaled, watching her reflection in the polished steel. This was the cost of power: lies wrapped in kindness, loyalty sacrificed for strategy.

Her phone buzzed—a secured message from Emily:

"Buffalo confirms contact. 3PM safehouse. Bring your go bag."

Clara straightened her shoulders. The game was moving. And she, like every ambitious woman who'd ever had to choose between truth and survival, would play to win.

The retinal scanner flashed green as Clara pressed her palm against the biometric lock. The safehouse door hissed open, revealing a war room humming with quiet intensity. The air smelled of espresso and ozone—the scent of sleepless strategizing and overclocked technology.

Emily stood before a floating holographic display, her military-straight posture silhouetted against swirling data streams. The projection showed a rotating model of Earth, with a blinking red dot over Antarctica. Clara's stomach tightened. She read the caption under that dot:

"Detected quantum satellite array."

Sarah and Linda flanked Emily, their faces lit by the cold blue glow. Nancy paced behind them, her usual composed elegance replaced by restless energy. The moment Clara stepped inside, four pairs of eyes locked onto her with predator focus.

"We intercepted him." Emily's voice cut through the hum of servers. She swiped a hand through the hologram, expanding a transcript log. "Buffalo Unit's been tailing Ethan since Central Park. They piggybacked on South Pole Station's quantum satellite to decrypt his last BLAND transmission."

Clara moved closer, her designer boots silent on the soundproofed flooring. The transcript floated before her:

"BLAND OPERATIVE 227 (TO ETHAN):

Priority shift. Rose is now primary extraction target. No force authorized—persuasion only. She must come willingly."

A chill spider-walked down Clara's spine. "Extraction target." Like she was some relic to be acquired.

"No threats?" Clara traced the glowing text with a manicured finger. "No ultimatums?"

Emily's smile was razor-thin. "They're being… unusually polite." She tapped another command. The hologram shifted to show Ethan's apartment—every angle covered by Buffalo's hidden cams. There he was, pacing like a caged animal, running hands through his disheveled hair.

Linda leaned in, her diamond earrings catching the light. "They want you 'specifically', Clara. Not just any ROWFIR."

Nancy stopped pacing. "Why?"

Sarah crossed her arms, her NYPD badge glinting. "That's what we need to—"

The hologram suddenly flashed crimson. An alert pulsed:

"QUANTUM SIGNATURE DETECTED – NEW TRANSMISSION DECRYPTING"

Emily's fingers flew across the interface. The screen resolved into a video feed—grainy but clear enough to make out a cavernous space with vaulted ceilings. And in the center...

Clara's breath caught.

Three female-looking figures sat atop golden daises, motionless as statues. Their faces were obscured by intricate metal veils, their draped gowns shimmering with what looked like "embedded circuitry". Around them, men moved in precise patterns—kneeling, offering trays, never touching, never speaking.

"The so-called goddesses," Emily muttered. "Buffalo's been trying to ID them for days."

Then—a voice. Distorted, genderless, emanating from the video:

"CLARA ROSE POSSESSES UNIQUE... COMPATIBILITY. BRING HER TO THE TEMPLE."

The screen went black.

Silence swallowed the room. Clara's pulse roared in her ears. "Compatibility?" With "what"?

Nancy was the first to speak. "That wasn't a request. It was a 'diagnosis'."

Sarah's hand hovered near her sidearm. "We can't let them have Clara."

"No." Clara's voice surprised even herself. She stepped into the hologram's glow, watching light refract through her wine-dark nails. "Let's give BLAND what they want."

Four stunned faces turned to her.

"You can't be serious," Linda breathed.

Emily met Clara's gaze. "I can plant a tracker in your bone

marrow. The new nano-tech Buffalo's been developed." She smiled, with zipped lips. The room exhaled. Emily's eyes glittered with something between pride and terror.

Somewhere beneath Antarctica, a quantum satellite blinked.

The game had just changed.

The next day, predawn light painted JFK's runways in shades of gunmetal and gold as Clara boarded the private jet, her leather carry-on containing everything she'd need for the most dangerous performance of her life. Emily followed, her crisp military posture never wavering despite the 18-hour flight ahead.

"Singapore's just a pitstop," Emily reminded her, buckling into the plush seat. "Changi Airport is the closest civilized gateway to BLAND's border. We'll regroup there before sending you into the lion's den."

The flight passed in a blur of strategy briefings and stolen naps. Clara woke as the plane banked over Singapore's jewel-toned skyline, the morning sun setting Marina Bay's towers ablaze. Even from the air, the city hummed with meticulous order—a stark contrast to the untamed mystery awaiting her beyond its borders.

(Changi Naval Base, 14:00 Local Time) The scent of saltwater and jet fuel hung heavy as Emily guided Clara through the secured gates of RSS Singapura. Seven women stood at attention on the aircraft carrier's deck, their silhouettes backlit by the equatorial sun.

"Meet your shadow team," Emily announced.

Clara took in the warriors before her:

- Aiyana, her dark braids threaded with silver, eyes sharp as a hawk's

- Kaya, fingers drumming a silent rhythm against her thigh—a sniper's restless energy

- Winona, whose quiet presence radiated the calm of endless tundra

- Nokomis, the oldest, with laugh lines that belied her lethal precision

- Tayanita, compact and coiled like a spring

- Kateri, her posture radiating quiet devotion to duty

- Aponi, who stepped forward at Emily's nod

"This is Lieutenant Aponi," Emily announced, her grip steady on the warrior's shoulder. "When things go dark—and they will—she's your ghost in the machine. Give her three minutes in any city, and she'll chart an exit route even the rats don't know about."

Aponi met Clara's gaze, her eyes sharp with the quiet confidence of someone who'd slipped through borders like smoke. "We specialize in making the impossible disappear."

Clara extended her hand. "I'm in your care, Lieutenant."

Aponi's grip was warm but firm. "We'll paint you a backdoor out of hell itself if needed, ma'am."

The hallway stretched long and silent, lit with soft overhead panels that cast a gentle sheen across the polished concrete floors. The air inside the military airport had a charged stillness to it—clean, sterile, but humming with the quiet hum of systems always awake, always alert.

Emily walked beside Clara at an even pace, her boots making no more sound than a whisper on the floor. Her presence was composed, focused, as if even in this moment of calm, she remained in sync with a deeper rhythm—the kind bred only by years of command.

As they moved, Clara's eyes were drawn to the wall displays lining the corridor—glass-encased lockers, each housing a pair of gloves unlike anything she'd ever seen. They were beautiful in a brutal, functional way. Sleek, high-tech, and unmistakably designed for war.

The gloves were shaped for a woman's hand—narrow at the wrist, articulated with seamless joints, but armored with intricate plating. The knuckles were reinforced with darkened steel, each curve molded to absorb impact. Over the fingertips, she noticed what looked like metal caps—nail guards—some tipped with shimmering diamond-like edges, catching the hallway lights like stars trapped in stone.

Clara slowed, staring.

"They're not just gloves," Emily said, sensing her curiosity before Clara could voice it. She stopped beside one of the cases and gave a small, knowing smile. "They're weapons."

Clara raised her eyebrows. "For punching?"

Emily chuckled softly, but it didn't quite reach her eyes. "These are integrated combat gauntlets. Emergency-use only—usually. They're calibrated to sync with our power armor systems. Some are layered with a diamond-carbide alloy at the nails—sharper than scalpels. And the knuckles can crack reinforced bone if needed."

Clara leaned in, studying the fine wiring that traced the interior like veins.

"But it's what you don't see," Emily continued, her voice lower now, "that makes them lethal."

She tapped the glass near one set, its inner lining glowing faintly beneath the surface. "Each glove is threaded with microtubes. When worn with our suits, they work in tandem to regulate chemical release throughout the armor—designed specifically for female soldiers with active Firen abilities."

Clara turned to her, still trying to piece it together. "You mean… they fire on order?"

Emily confirmed. "We found out that Women who process Firen can manage it with technique. It doesn't have to be sudden outbreaks—it's a chemical reaction tied to emotion. Like a wise person who knows how to regulate her emotions, these suits help channel that power. Control it. Weaponize it."

She glanced down the hallway, her expression sharpening. "BLAND knows it. That's why they're afraid of us. Why they try to strip it away."

Clara felt a flicker deep in her chest—not fear, not awe, but something deeper. Something ancestral.

She looked again at the gloves behind the glass. They were elegant, deadly. Not the crude tools of male warfare, but the precise, intentional armor of women who had refused to be erased.

"They're beautiful," Clara said quietly.

"They're ours," Emily replied. "Every inch designed by women, for women. We don't just survive war, Clara. We *reshape* it."

The words hung in the air like prophecy.

And for the first time in a long while, Clara felt something stirring beneath her skin—something molten, something ready.

At the private terminal, Emily pulled Clara into a rare, fierce embrace. "Remember," she murmured into Clara's hair, "BLAND plays the long game. So do we. Good luck, my friend."

Then she was gone, leaving Clara with seven warriors and a boarding pass that might as well have read 'Destination: Unknown'.

The cabin lights dimmed as they crossed into BLAND airspace. Clara lifted the window shade—

—and caught her breath.

Where Singapore had been all glass and steel precision, this land sprawled in ochre and rust, a living tapestry of dunes and rock formations unchanged for millennia. The runway appeared like a mirage, a black ribbon laid across the desert by some unseen hand.

Aponi's voice cut through the plane's silence. "Jeru welcomes you."

The capital rose in the distance, its skyline a surreal marriage of ancient ziggurats and obsidian towers. Somewhere in that city waited answers about why BLAND wanted her—and what "compatibility" truly meant.

Clara smoothed her linen blazer, her fingers brushing the nano-tracker embedded near the lapel. She'd walked into boardrooms and galas a hundred times before.

But never into the belly of the beast.

It landed smoothly.

The aircraft cabin hummed with silent tension as Clara sat motionless in the front seat, her fingers tracing the edge of her armrests. Behind her, the seven warriors of Emily's elite unit moved with the quiet synchronicity of a well-oiled machine. They were more than soldiers—they were artists of survival.

- Aiyana, the linguist, could unravel dialects like threads from a tapestry.

- Kaya, their electronic warfare specialist, could blind an enemy's satellites with a flick of her wrist.

- Winona, the silent shadow, was a ghost in close-quarters combat.

- Nokomis, their surveillance oracle, saw patterns where others saw chaos.

- Tayanita, small but lethal, could disappear into any crowd.

- Kateri, their medic, carried both sutures and secrets.

- Aponi, their escape architect, could carve a path through hell itself.

They didn't just move—they flowed, a single entity forged in fire and precision.

The aircraft door hissed open, and the desert surged in—a wave of dry, golden heat laced with the faintest whisper of jasmine. Clara rose, her polished boots clicking against the metal stairs as she descended into the light.

The airstrip was nothing like she'd imagined.

No terminals. No crowds. Just an open expanse of sun-bleached stone, cradled between sandstone ridges that rose like the ribs of some ancient beast. The air shimmered with heat, distorting the horizon.

And then she saw 'them'.

A dozen men in immaculate navy-blue uniforms stood at attention, their silver insignias catching the sun. Their posture was flawless, their expressions unreadable—a living mural of discipline and control.

At their forefront stood two figures:

A man, tall and broad-shouldered, his presence both commanding and serene.

A woman, petite and draped in flowing silk, her dark eyes holding depths Clara couldn't yet fathom.

The man stepped forward with the grace of a desert prince, his bow deep and deliberate, the embroidered hem of his kaftan whispering against the wind. The scent of amber and oud curled in the air around him, rich and intoxicating.

"Welcome to the United BLAND," he said, his voice like aged whiskey—smooth, with an undercurrent of strength that spoke of years wielding both diplomacy and blade. "You must be Clara. I am Shietar, Prime Minister of this land." His dark eyes, sharp as a falcon's, held hers for a breath before he turned slightly, extending a hand toward the woman beside him. "And this is my wife, Yolanda."

Yolanda was a vision of effortless elegance, her flowing abaya adorned with delicate gold embroidery that caught the light like scattered stars. Her hands, sheathed in smooth golden gloves—the kind worn by noblewomen who never toiled but always ruled—rested gracefully at her waist. The gloves fit snugly, yet there was something peculiar about them: her fingers appeared shorter than one might expect, as if the fine silk had been tailored to conceal rather than reveal.

Her smile was warm, the kind that could put a guest at ease—but her gaze? That was what unsettled Clara. It was the look of a woman who had navigated courts and intrigues, who could unravel a soul with a single glance and weigh its worth without a word.

"We've heard so much about you," Yolanda murmured, her voice like silk gliding over steel. The bangles at her wrists chimed softly as she lifted a gloved hand, the gesture both welcoming and assessing. "It's rare to meet someone who walks between worlds as you do. Like a desert fox at home in both shadow and sun."

Clara's eyes flickered, just for an instant, to those golden-clad fingers—too short, too deliberate. A flaw? A secret? Or a carefully crafted distraction?

Her pulse remained steady, though the weight of their attention pressed against her like the dry, heavy heat of a midsummer wind. She inclined her head, just enough to show respect but not submission. "I'm grateful for the invitation," she replied, her tone polished, diplomatic. Behind her, the seven warriors—each a silent storm of coiled strength—fanned out in a protective arc, their presence a quiet reminder: she was not a woman who walked into the unknown unprepared.

The air between them thrummed with unspoken challenge, the kind that lingers before a game of senet, before the first move is made.

Shietar gestured toward a line of sleek, sand-resistant vehicles. "We'll take you to your quarters. Rest. Tonight, we show you Jeru as it truly is." His smile deepened. "The King will receive you tomorrow. But first… let us welcome you properly."

As the convoy glided away from the airstrip, Clara glanced back at the jet—her last tether to the world she knew. Ahead, Jeru rose from the desert like a dream, its golden domes and ivory towers glowing under the relentless sun.

Beautiful.

Mysterious.

Dangerous.

Aponi leaned in, her voice a whisper. "First impressions?"

Clara didn't take her eyes off the city. "Either the friendliest reception committee I've ever met…" She paused. "Or the most elegant trap."

The desert wind sighed against the windows, carrying secrets older than time.

And Clara?

She was just getting started.

CHAPTER 13: SHORT FINGERS

The vehicle that awaited Clara and her warriors was a monstrous thing—gleaming black with gold filigree, its engine a low, throaty growl like a desert beast stirring from slumber. As it glided through the winding streets of BLAND's capital, Clara leaned her head to the tinted window, watching the city unfold like a living tapestry.

The landscape was something out of an old tale—towering minarets crowned with sapphire domes, market squares bustling with vendors under striped awnings, and canals that shimmered like ribbons of liquid silver. It reminded her of the Aladdin movies she'd watched as a child, but this was no fantasy. This was real. And so were the women.

Everywhere she looked, they moved with effortless grace, draped in silken robes that whispered against the cobblestones. Their hands, sheathed in gloves of every hue—ruby red, emerald green, twilight violet—fluttered like exotic birds as they bartered, laughed, or carried baskets of spices on their hips. But it was the gloves that held Clara's attention. Always the gloves.

Soon they arrived. The grand doors swung open to admit them, the afternoon air swirling in with the scent of blooming jasmine. Shietar and Yolanda offered a deep, synchronized bow of perfect respect. With a final, graceful gesture, they withdrew, leaving the esteemed guests in the capable hands of the waiting servants—the silent transition as flawless as a well-rehearsed dance. Their accommodations were a mirage made solid—white stone arches draped in jasmine vines, courtyards where fountains sang, and pools so clear they mirrored the sky. Yet beneath the luxury, Clara's team moved with precision, their instincts sharp as blades.

- Kaya crouched near a gilded table, her fingers flying over a holographic communicator. "Emily, do you copy? We need a signal boost." Static hissed back but no signal yet.

- Aiyana had already raided the shelves, her sharp eyes scanning ancient texts. "Their language is a mix of proto-Arabic and something… older. And their ideology? 'Purity through sacrifice.' Charming."

- Winona and Nokomis prowled the perimeter, testing locks, tracing sightlines from the latticed windows. "Too many blind spots," Winona muttered.

- Aponi held a scanner no larger than a coin, its hologram spiraling outward. "Building is mapped. So's the city." She tapped the display. "Interesting. There's a subterranean network beneath us. Tunnels."

- Tayanita never left Clara's shadow, her hand resting on the hilt of her dagger. Ready. Always ready.

Then Kateri spoke, her voice low. "Clara. Their fingers." She held up her own hand, measuring. "The women here? Their digits are an inch shorter than the human average. Could be another mutation. And the men—" She glanced at the bustling streets beyond the window. "They don't fear Firen. At all."

A knock, soft but deliberate, echoed through the room like a ripple across still water. The heavy wooden door creaked open, and three women stepped inside in silence. They moved with the practiced grace of ritual—balanced, purposeful—each carrying a silver tray with care so precise it bordered on reverence.

On one tray, ripe figs glistened under a glaze of honey, their skins split like velvet secrets. Another held porcelain cups of amber tea, steam rising in elegant spirals, rich with the scent of clove and cardamom. The third tray cradled a stack of warm, round bread, its crust blistered and golden, the kind of bread made from ancient recipes and handed down like prayer.

Their gloves were the first thing Clara noticed—ivory-white, flawless, extending nearly to the elbow. Pristine. Not the sort of gloves worn for fashion or modesty, but for containment. Or protection.

Tayanita, ever watchful, moved before anyone else could speak. She caught the wrist of the closest servant—a woman with downcast eyes and a mouth pressed into a careful line. Her gloved hand trembled slightly beneath Tayanita's grip.

"Why the gloves?" Tayanita asked, voice low but laced with steel.

The servant flinched. Her gaze darted, not toward an escape route, but toward the marble floor—as if answers might be carved in stone. "I cannot answer," she said softly.

Then, with the swiftness of smoke dispersing through air, she slipped free and was gone—leaving behind a ghost of perfume and unease.

The silence stretched, taut as wire.

It was Kaya who broke it, turning toward the others with her tablet cradled in one arm and a glint of both excitement and concern in her eyes. "I've got good news and bad news," she said, tapping rapidly as screens flickered to life beneath her fingers.

"The good news is I've managed to connect to the local internet nodes and shortwave radio frequencies. I'm already collecting and analyzing behavioral data, speech patterns, media tone. We're starting to map the social terrain here in BLAND—what people say, what they fear, what they *won't* say."

There was a beat, and then the shift.

"The bad news?" Kaya's voice lost its lilt. "I can't reach our satellite. Not a blip. I've pinged every channel. It's like we're under a dome. If I had to guess, I'd say BLAND's built satellite shielding—some kind of atmospheric scrambling tech. We're cut off. No contact with Emily. No outside comms. We're on our own."

A hush settled over the room like fog. Even the bread seemed to steam more quietly.

Clara looked at the others. The tension in their bodies was unmistakable. Shoulders drawn. Eyes alert. The quiet kind of fear—the kind that didn't scream, but settled low in the gut, cold and heavy.

Then, the door opened again.

This time, it was Lan.

She entered with the quiet command of someone used to being heard without raising her voice. Her robe shimmered in the candlelight, deep blue like crushed lapis, embroidered with thread so fine it caught the glow like stars on water. Her hands were bare. Her smile—serene, knowing, and somehow older than her face—gave nothing away.

"The Mother Goddess awaits you," she said. "When you are ready."

Her voice had the weight of ceremony, like a bell tolling across a distant valley.

Clara exchanged glances with Tayanita and Kateri. No one needed to say what they were all thinking. The air was changing. The road behind them was gone, swallowed by choices already made.

"There's no turning back," Clara said, her voice steady. She stepped forward.

"Let's go."

And the women followed her—into the unknown, into the heart

of BLAND's secrets, into whatever waited beyond that fine door.

The temple rose before them like a gilded dream, its arches catching the late afternoon sun and scattering flecks of gold across the marble steps. Every pillar was a living masterpiece, twined with jasmine and crimson roses that perfumed the air with their heady sweetness. As Clara ascended the stairs, the scent of frankincense curled around her—warm, sacred, cloying. Beneath it lingered something darker, something metallic. Blood or incense? She couldn't tell.

Inside, the hall stretched vast and shimmering, the walls inlaid with mosaics of women with perfect, gloved hands raised in prayer. The air hummed with whispered hymns, the sound drifting like smoke from hidden alcoves. And there, upon a dais bathed in honeyed light, sat the Mother Goddess.

She was radiance incarnate. Her gown, molten gold, pooled around her like liquid sunlight, each fold sewn with tiny pearls that caught the candlelight. Her face was veiled—not by cloth, but by a cascade of living petals, tiny white blossoms that trembled with every breath. When she spoke, her voice was a balm, soft as rosewater, smooth as poisoned honey.

"Welcome, Clara." A gloved hand gestured to the silk cushions arranged before her. "Please, sit. Share tea with me."

Clara knelt, the cushions yielding beneath her. Tayanita and Kateri flanked her, their postures taut as bowstrings. The goddess lifted the teapot—an ornate thing of enamel and gold—her movements deliberate. Her fingers, even gloved, were unmistakably short, the fabric straining over what should have been knuckles.

She poured the tea with ceremonial grace, the steam twisting into phantom shapes between them. A young girl around 6-7 years old came out from behind the curtains and served the tea cups to Clara and her staff.

Then, with a slow, almost theatrical pause, the goddess set down her cup. "You must be uncomfortable in this heat," her voice dripping with false sympathy. With deliberate care, she peeled off one golden glove, then the other.

The truth beneath was grotesque.

Where fingertips should have been, there were only smooth, rounded caps of gold fused to the flesh, the skin around them puckered with old scars. No nails. No grooves. Just cold, unyielding metal, as if her very bones had been dipped in gilt and left to harden.

Clara's stomach lurched. **This wasn't mutation. This was butchery.**

"You must be curious," the goddess said, extending her disfigured hand without shame. The gold tips caught the light, gleaming like a perverse badge of honor. "In BLAND, we call it the Purification. A sacred rite, performed before a girl's first blood—before she can ever produce Firen."

She lifted the teapot again, the metal fingers clinking against porcelain. "We believe Firen is evil incarnate. A corruption of the soul." Her veiled face tilted, the petals shivering. "And our mission—" Here, her voice dropped, saccharine and sinister, "—is to liberate the world from it. So all may know Purity."

The teacup in Clara's hand trembled. Not just from fear.

But from rage.

A knowing smile touched the gilded woman's lips, not quite reaching her enigmatic eyes. "A mind as sharp as yours will not easily surrender to a new reality," she said, her voice a low, melodic hum that seemed to carry the weight of centuries. Her words were a compliment, yet they hung in the air, laced with a hidden significance that Clara couldn't quite decipher—a secret just beyond her grasp.

The woman leaned forward, the intricate gold of her gown whispering with the movement. "But even the brightest minds need rest. Try to find sleep tonight," she urged, her tone softening into something that almost resembled genuine concern. "Tomorrow awaits you, and it promises to be… momentous." With a graceful, almost dismissive wave of her hand, she summoned a young attendant from the shadows. "See our guest to her chambers."

CHAPTER 14: THE KING'S GAMBIT

Clara barely slept. She kept replaying her trip so far and wondering what the goddess's words mean. Before Clara could find a clue, the summons came at dawn—a scrap of vellum sealed with black wax, delivered by a stone-faced courier whose gloves were the color of dried blood.

"His Majesty requests your presence," the man had said, his voice flat. "You may bring your... companions."

Clara had read between the lines. A command, not an invitation.

The military base sprawled across the desert like a sleeping scorpion; its low-slung bunkers half-buried in the dunes. Heat shimmered above the sand, distorting the horizon into a liquid mirage. Clara and the Buffalo Sisters moved as one—seven shadows flanking her, their footfalls silent, their eyes missing nothing.

Beneath a sky bleached pale by the relentless sun, the training yard stretched before them like an ancient arena. The air shimmered with heat, carrying whispers of cinnamon and gunpowder from distant barracks. At its epicenter stood King Malik, a silhouette carved from shadow and gold against the vast emptiness.

The wind played with the edges of his black keffiyeh, the fine fabric dancing like a living thing around his strong features. No crown weighed upon his brow today - only the authority in his stance spoke of royalty. The desert sun had kissed his skin to a deep bronze, and when he turned to face them, his eyes gleamed like polished obsidian catching firelight.

"Clara," he greeted, his voice a rich timbre that carried effortlessly across the space between them. He spread his hands in a gesture that might have been hospitality, were it not for the dangerous curve of his smile - the expression of a leopard tolerating visitors in its territory. "How fortuitous to find guests who don't wilt in the heat. I've always appreciated an audience with... spine."

A slow, deliberate smile graced Clara's lips, a carefully constructed mask of composure. "I'm flattered," she said, her voice steady as she held the king's penetrating gaze. She willed every ounce of her being to project a cool, unshakeable confidence, a direct challenge to the authority that radiated from him. Yet, betrayed by a single tell, her trembled fingers, shimmering like a captured heartbeat.

Malik's eyes, dark and perceptive, caught the minute tremor. A spark of pure amusement ignited within them, not of mockery, but of genuine intrigue. He had expected fear, but this performance of defiance was far more entertaining. "The pleasure is mine, Clara." he replied, her name a low, intimate rumble in the space between them. He recognized her game and seemed inclined to play.

"I thought a proper welcome was in order," he continued, offering his arm not as a request, but as a command woven in silk. "I've prepared a... private exhibition. Consider it your first lesson in the aesthetics of this world." He guided her toward a lavish carpet unfurled like a river of crimson and gold, its path leading their eyes to the vast, unforgiving desert that stretched beyond the palace walls—a stark contrast to the opulence he commanded.

The weapons display unfolded like a carefully choreographed dance. Attendants in flowing indigo robes moved with silent precision, unveiling each marvel as the king narrated their virtues with the pride of a master artisan showing his finest creations.

First came the Mecha Suit, emerging from its protective casing with an almost liquid grace. The surface shimmered like a mirage, shifting between mother-of-pearl iridescence and mercury's reflective depth as it caught the light. King Malik approached it with something approaching reverence, his gloved hand trailing along the armored contours with intimate familiarity.

"Behold our second skin," he murmured, his fingers tracing the suit's seamless joints. "Forged in our deepest laboratories, this marvel laughs at Firen release and shrugs off radiation storms. Our warriors could stroll through the seven hells wearing nothing but this." His dark eyes flicked to Clara, amusement glinting in their depths. "A pity we haven't yet tailored one for more... delicate frames."

The attendants rotated the suit slowly, revealing how light played across its surface - one moment matte as desert stone, the next gleaming like wet ink. The very air around it seemed to hum with contained energy, a sleeping giant awaiting its wearer's command.

Around them, the desert wind carried the distant sound of wind chimes from some unseen pavilion, mingling with the faint metallic scent of the displayed armaments. The king stood at the center of it all, his presence as commanding as the war machine he presented, every inch the desert hawk surveying his domain.

And then, the attendants parted like curtains before a performance, revealing the second marvel of King Malik's arsenal. The Dundrum Armor stood sentinel upon an obsidian dais, its matte-black exoskeleton drinking in the sunlight like a void given form. The surface wasn't merely dark—it seemed to swallow light itself, etched with barely-visible geometric patterns that shimmered like heat waves when viewed from the corner of the eye.

The helmet's visor slanted like a serpent's gaze, its crimson optical sensors pulsing with a slow, rhythmic glow that mirrored breathing. As they approached, the armor's shoulder plates shifted almost imperceptibly, the motion whisper-quiet—not mechanical, but organic, like a great cat adjusting its stance.

"Ah, our desert scorpion," King Malik crooned, circling the armor with proprietary pride. His ceremonial robes whispered across the sand as he gestured to the admiral standing at attention beside it. The military man's fingers danced across the gauntlet's control interface with the practiced ease of a musician touching his favorite instrument.

A sound like crystallized lightning cracked the air as the laser knife ignited—a blade of pure cobalt energy that hummed with contained fury. The air around it shimmered with displaced heat, distorting the view of the desert beyond. The king extended a hand toward the vibrating blade, close enough for its azure glow to paint his rings with liquid light, but not close enough to burn.

"Twenty meters of precision," he murmured, his voice thick with admiration. "It reads the density of what it cuts—adjusting frequency to slice through reinforced bulkheads or…" His eyes flicked to Clara's throat briefly before continuing, "…more delicate materials with equal grace."

A pregnant silence followed. Then, with the barest arch of one perfect eyebrow, the king gave the unspoken command.

"Show them," he breathed.

The admiral's fingers flew across the controls. For a heartbeat—nothing. Then the armor came alive with terrifying grace.

It moved not with the jerky motions of machinery, but with the lethal elegance of a predator. The laser knife whirled in a blinding arc, tracing a burning afterimage in the air. Before the eye could register the movement, the armor's wrist snapped forward. A projectile of condensed light screamed across the training yard—a comet's tail of blue fire that found its mark with unerring accuracy.

The distant target dummy didn't just explode—it vaporized in a corona of white-hot sparks, the sand beneath it fusing instantly to glass. The shockwave sent ripples through the desert floor, kicking up a ring of dust that expanded like some ancient summoning circle.

Through the settling debris, the Buffalo Sisters stood unwavering—though Clara felt the minute tension in Kateri's stance beside her, the way her fingers had drifted to the tribal dagger at her hip. The king noted this too, his lips curving in a smile that didn't reach his eyes.

"Magnificent, isn't it?" he mused, watching the last embers of destruction fade into the desert wind. "Technology and artistry, married in perfect harmony." The dying light of the energy weapon reflecting in his dark eyes. He turned to Kateri in a provocative tone, "Tell me, warrior woman—does your homeland boast such... beautiful innovations?"

The unspoken challenge hung between them, as palpable as the ozone scent of discharged energy weapons. Around them, the desert held its breath.

Though the air crackled with tension, Kateri and all the Buffalo sisters were islands of absolute calm. Their spines were steel rods; shoulders set in a line so precise it seemed drawn by a surveyor's tool. That was not merely a military pose; it was the embodiment of a will forged in discipline and unshakable resolve. Their silence was not empty, but profoundly loud— a proud, defiant testament to their strength that echoed more powerfully than any shouted protest could. In the stillness, the sisters were not just holding a position; they were holding their grounds, dignity, and power, daring anyone to question it.

King Malik's laughter unfurled across the training grounds like rare silk unwinding - a deep, mellifluous sound that somehow made the desert heat feel colder. His amber eyes remained watchful as moonlit dunes, the mirth never reaching their calculating depths. "Enough theatrics," he declared with an elegant wave of his hand, the jewels on his fingers catching fire in the sunlight. At his gesture, the mighty armor hissed into submission, its glowing blades dimming like dying stars. "We mustn't overwhelm our honored guests," he purred, the words dripping with false chivalry.

With the grace of a desert fox leading prey to its den, Malik guided Clara toward an ornate pedestal of polished black marble. Upon it rested a wooden chest so exquisite it seemed stolen from a sultan's treasure vault - its sandalwood surface carved with intertwining pomegranate vines. Each leaf inlaid with mother-of-pearl that shimmered like mirages on hot sand. Too beautiful, too delicate for the horror it contained.

The king produced a slender key from his robes (the metal warm from resting against his chest) and unlocked the chest with a lover's tenderness. The velvet-lined interior cradled six projectiles that gleamed like liquid mercury. These were no common bullets - they were masterworks of malice, each casing slender as a woman's finger and etched with tiny, writhing sigils that seemed to move when stared at too long.

"Ah, our alchemical poetry," Malik breathed, lifting one bullet between thumb and forefinger as if examining a rare jewel. The sunlight revealed the capsule's translucent core where amber-hued chemicals swirled lazily. "A... tribute to your Firen, if you will." His voice took on the cadence of a storyteller weaving dark fairy tales. "A reversed bioengineering that target female bodies. The first kiss brings numbness - a lover's mercy. Then comes the slow dance of fire in the veins." He rotated the bullet slowly, watching the poison catch the light. "Seven days to contemplate one's mortality as the burn spreads. Seven sunrises to make peace with the gods before..." His plush lips formed a silent 'pop', the sound obscenely gentle. "But surely a woman of your wisdom needs no crude explanation."

Clara's palms betrayed her—a fine sheen of moisture glistening against her skin despite the desert's arid breath. She commanded her lungs to move steadily, each inhalation measured, each exhalation controlled, but the king's hawk-like gaze missed nothing.

His lips curved into a smile that didn't reach his eyes, the expression of a predator savoring the tremor of its prey. "Don't fret, my dear Clara," he murmured, closing the distance between them with the languid grace of a sand panther. Now near enough that his scent enveloped her—the heady spice of saffron clinging to his robes, undercut by the acrid tang of gun oil, a dissonant harmony of luxury and violence.

A gloved hand lifted, the supple leather whispering through the air just above her bare fingers. Close enough that she felt the disturbance in the space between them, yet never making contact. The restraint itself was a provocation.

"These... toys," he continued, his voice a velvet-wrapped blade, "aren't meant for you." His gaze dropped to her hands, lingering on the delicate bones of her wrists, the unblemished skin. "Not when you possess such... exquisite hands." The words slithered between them, weighted with implication. "So soft. So very... intact."

A frisson of ice traced Clara's spine—not from the evening chill creeping across the desert, but from the unspoken threat coiled beneath his honeyed words. The way his attention lingered on her fingers spoke volumes; in this kingdom of mutilated women, her unaltered hands marked her as both outsider and potential victim.

Around them, the Buffalo Sisters tensed, their protective formation tightening like a noose. Kateri's fingers twitched toward her blade, the movement infinitesimal but telling. The king noted it all, his smile deepening, savoring the tension thickening the air between them.

In that moment, Clara understood something chilling—

something no blade, no bullet, no wall of iron could match. The true weapon here was not locked in the ornate box at the king's side, nor hidden in the silent rows of polished armor that stood like frozen sentinels in the desert.

It was something far quieter. Far more dangerous.

It was the dawning horror that bloomed cold in her chest: in BLAND, even kindness could kill.

A compliment here was never just a pleasantry—it was a test. A snare. A disguised command dressed in velvet.

"Don't worry, my dear friend from far away," the king said, his smile smooth, practiced—almost fatherly. "BLAND will treat you just *alright*."

His eyes met hers with the weight of something unreadable, and for one breathless moment, Clara felt as though he were peering through her skin into her very marrow.

"You must be overwhelmed," he added, voice dipping into concern that felt just a touch too rehearsed. "How about some good rest for tonight? We'll talk more in the morning."

It sounded gentle enough. But in that honeyed tone, Clara heard the finality of a closed door.

She returned to her temporary quarters with the others. Her boots echoed against the stone floors like distant gunshots. No one spoke much. Work station occasionally beeps but no signals from Emily yet. The silence between them felt dense, as though they all sensed the noose tightening, but couldn't yet name it aloud.

In her chamber, the security from her sisters nearby wasn't enough to quiet her mind. Her bed, though warm and well-made, felt foreign. Watching the candlelight tremble on the walls, Clara lay still for a long time—her thoughts a slow churn of strategy, doubt, and something close to dread.

Eventually, sleep claimed her—but it was the brittle kind,

shallow and uneasy.

Because now she knew: in BLAND, the danger didn't always announce itself with a sword.

Sometimes, it smiled.

CHAPTER 15: CROCODILE'S TEAR

The desert wept.

Rain—rare as mercy in this parched land—poured in silver veils over BLAND, transforming the dust-choked streets into something almost sacred. The sky, so often a hard dome of unbroken heat, had cracked open at last. The earth drank deeply, greedily, as if it, too, had longed to feel something real.

It felt like the gods were grieving.

By morning, the air was thick with the scent of renewal and sorrow—wet stone, bruised blossoms, and the deep, stirring musk of damp soil. *Petrichor*, her mother used to call it. The word came back to Clara like a whispered memory, carried on the breath of the storm. She hadn't heard it in years, yet now it unfurled within her like a lullaby she'd nearly forgotten.

Lan arrived after breakfast, her dark cloak heavy with the weight of rain, though she smiled as if the storm had blessed her. She said the tour had been granted by decree of the Mother Goddess herself—an honor, a gesture of trust.

Clara didn't trust gestures.

Still, she followed, her shadow-bodyguard— Tayanita —never more than two steps behind.

They stopped before a grand sandstone structure carved with delicate patterns of flame and feather. **The Girls' Institute of Purity**. A name that left a bitter taste in Clara's mouth even before they crossed the threshold.

She paused under the arched entryway, her eyes tracing the rivulets of rain carving uneven lines down the timeworn walls. The droplets moved like tears over a stoic face—resigned, uncomplaining, ancient.

A shiver stirred beneath her ribs. This place held secrets. She could feel it in the silence that clung to its stones, in the hush behind the rain.

Somewhere deep in her, a memory flickered: the soft hum of her mother's voice as she watered garden beds back home, bare hands in rich soil, speaking of healing, of honesty, of how the earth knows what is real.

And now, Clara stood on foreign soil, with the ghost of that memory pressing gently against her heart, unsure if she'd ever walk through that garden again.

Inside, the institute was a paradox of beauty and cruelty.

Marble floors gleamed under crystal chandeliers; their light softened by delicate silk shades. Young girls in identical ivory dresses moved through the halls with practiced grace, their gloved hands folded neatly at their waists. Clara noted the way their eyes flickered to her bare fingers—some with curiosity, others with something like fear.

A matron, her own gloves embroidered with golden thread, guided Clara through the facility. "At nine years old," the woman explained, her voice polished smooth as the pearls at her throat, "each girl undergoes the **Rite of Purification**. A spiritual elder guides them through the ceremony. It's a great honor."

Clara's stomach twisted. She had seen the results of that "honor" in the Mother Goddess's gilded stumps.

They passed a sunlit room where infants slept in identical cribs. "Mothers may visit once a month," the matron said, adjusting a blanket with impersonal efficiency.

"That's really short time for a baby to be with her mother." Clara said in concerns.

"Attachment weakens the spirit. At day three, the child belongs to BLAND." the matron explained like she was fully committed to it.

A tiny fist waved in the air, grasping at nothing. Clara wondered if the babe would dream of a voice she'd never know. Clara kept silent for the rest of the tour, since she felt sick of it.

That evening, King Malik summoned Clara to his private chamber. Outside, the rain still whispered against the stained-glass windows, each drop casting ribbons of fractured light that shimmered across the room—and across his face. For the first time, Malik didn't look like a ruler cloaked in iron certainty. He looked… human. Worn. Haunted.

When Clara and Tayanita arrived at the door to the king's chamber, he insisted on seeing Clara alone. Tayanita bristled at the idea, her concern written plainly in the set of her jaw. But Clara, drawn by a need to understand what lay behind the king's guarded eyes, chose to go. She promised Tayanita she'd be careful. Tayanita reluctantly agreed to wait just outside the heavy oak doors.

Inside, the chamber felt intimate in a way Clara hadn't expected. A fire burned low in the hearth, its warmth competing with the cool hush of the rain. Malik stood at a carved table, pouring wine into two slender goblets—himself. That alone startled her. Kings did not pour wine.

"You think our ways are cruel," he began, his voice low, like a story told too many times. He offered her a goblet, and as their fingers brushed, she felt the tremor in his hand. "But we are not monsters. We are desperate."

He looked up at her then, and in that moment, the veneer of power slipped. "Firen is a curse, Clara. My people live every day waiting for it to strike. Do you know what it's like to hear a father scream when her daughter first release ignites from within? To watch helplessly as a child boy burns—alive, screaming for a salvation no one can give?"

Clara didn't flinch, though the horror of his words sat heavy in her chest. "And cutting them—hurting them—this is your solution?"

His mask shattered. "I *hate* it," he whispered, raw as an open wound. His eyes shimmered, and a single tear escaped—genuine or manipulative, Clara couldn't yet tell. "But if there were another way…" He stepped closer, reaching for her hand with surprising tenderness. "With you, perhaps there could be."

She didn't move, didn't speak, though her heart thundered in her ribs.

"Stay," he murmured. "Be my queen. Help me build a legacy where our daughters will never know that pain. Where no little girl will ever be feared for what she carries inside her."

The offer lingered between them, thick and heavy like the air before a thunderclap. Outside, the storm rolled on—but inside, time held its breath.

Clara pulled away. "You mutilate children and call it salvation. Firen isn't evil—it's *life*. It's the power of nature, like the desert itself."

The king's expression hardened. "Think very carefully," he warned, though his voice remained soft. "Rest now. We'll speak tomorrow."

Chamber door opened slowly. A lady servant walked in, her eyes downcast, her manner too polite. "My lady," she murmured, "please allow me to show your way back to your room."

Clara hesitated for only a breath, then followed her out of the king's private chamber. The corridor was dim, lined with flickering sconces, and silent but for the fading patter of rain. She stepped into the hallway expecting to see Tayanita—loyal, unyielding Tayanita—standing at her post like a blade waiting to be drawn.

But she wasn't there.

Clara's steps slowed. She felt like walking into a trap. A prickle ran along her neck.

Something was wrong.

Clara's fingers twitched at her sides as she studied the servant's downcast face. The woman couldn't have been older than forty, but the way she carried herself—shoulders hunched forward, chin tucked nearly to her chest—made her seem both younger and more ancient at once. The flickering torchlight caught the frayed edges of her linen headscarf and the raw redness of knuckles that had spent too many years scrubbing floors.

"Excuse me. Where is Tayanita, the lady who were standing outside the chamber?" Clara asked, softening her tone just enough to seem less like a demand and more like a shared confidence between women.

The servant's eyes darted to the shadowed corridor behind them before answering. When she spoke, her voice was barely audible —a featherlight tremor of sound that seemed to dissolve in the air between them. "Sooorry. I... I do not know, my lady." Her fingers plucked nervously at the folds of her skirt, the fabric worn thin at the knees. "Your quarters are this way."

There was something in the way she said it—not just deference, but a quiet warning. The woman's gaze flickered meaningfully toward an alcove where the shadows moved just slightly too much for empty darkness. When Clara didn't immediately follow, the servant dared to meet her eyes for one fleeting second—just long enough for Clara to see the sheen of terrified tears clinging to her lashes—before bowing her head again and turning toward the hallway.

Every instinct screamed that this woman knew exactly where Tayanita was. And that whatever had happened was something she couldn't—or wouldn't—speak aloud in these echoing stone corridors where even the tapestries seemed to listen.

When she reached her quarters, the unease bloomed into a cold knot in her chest. The room looked as it always had—neat, orderly—but something vital was missing. It took her a moment to realize why the air felt hollow.

Tayanita's bed was untouched. Her weapons, usually laid with quiet precision near the footboard, was missing.

She's gone.

Before the ache of that thought could take root, the remaining Buffalo Sisters appeared like shadows drawn to a single flame. Their faces were grim.

Kaya stepped forward. "Lan was seen near the eastern gates just before dusk," she said, her voice edged with tension. "And the king's guards… they've doubled."

The meaning struck immediately. Clara's hand moved to the dagger strapped at her thigh, a familiar, silent reassurance. She looked at each of the women—their loyalty, their rage, their unspoken fear.

They were no longer guests here.

Clara took a steadying breath and told them everything—what the king had said, what he had offered. The twisted hope he dangled like a gilded noose.

Kateri's face hardened. "Obviously, the king is interested in you. But if you stay. He'll use you. Not as a queen. As a womb. A breeding vessel wrapped in silk and gold."

Suddenly, the heavy oak door creaked open with theatrical slowness, its ancient hinges groaning like a wounded animal. Lan glided into the room with the silent grace of a panther stalking its prey, her embroidered silk robes whispering against the marble floor. The temperature in the room seemed to drop several degrees as she entered, the air turning thin and brittle - as if the very atmosphere recoiled from her presence.

"My honored guests," Lan purred, her voice dripping with honeyed poison. She dipped into a shallow bow that managed to be both perfectly respectful and utterly condescending. "The King requests Clara's presence tomorrow before dinner." Her crimson lips curved into a smile that never reached her cold, calculating eyes.

Clara's hands clenched into fists at her sides, her nails biting into her palms. "Where is Tayanita?" she demanded, her voice sharp as a blade. "The warrior who was stationed outside these chambers?"

Lan's expression remained as smooth as polished jade. "My lady," she said with deliberate patience, "your bodyguard is quite safe… for now. You shall see her tomorrow." The unspoken threat hung heavy between them, as tangible as the gold threads in Lan's elaborate headdress.

"I want her returned immediately," Clara snapped, her patience evaporating like morning dew in the desert sun.

Lan's laugh was the tinkling of delicate wind chimes - beautiful and utterly soulless. "You are perfectly safe here, my dear," she cooed, as one might comfort a frightened child. "All in good time." With another infuriatingly perfect bow, she withdrew, leaving behind only the faint scent of sandalwood and betrayal.

The moment the door clicked shut, Clara exhaled sharply, her shoulders sagging momentarily before she straightened with renewed determination. She turned to Kateri, her eyes blazing with quiet fury.

"You were right," Clara admitted, her voice low and urgent. "They're treating us like prized animals in a gilded cage." She began pacing the length of the chamber, her boots sinking into the plush carpets. "It's time we planned our exit strategy." Kateri said and turned to Aponi.

Aponi stepped forward, her fingers already tracing invisible maps in the air. "I can have escape routes charted by morning," she offered, her voice steady with quiet confidence. "We could be ready to move tomorrow night."

"And the King's summons?" Winona asked from her post by the window, her fingers absently testing the edge of her dagger.

Clara paused at the ornate mirror, studying her reflection - the determined set of her jaw, the fire in her eyes. "We'll play along," she decided. "At least until we're certain of Tayanita's location." Her fingers brushed against the hidden pocket where she kept her most precious possession - a tiny compass from her homeland. "But make no mistake - we're leaving this gilded prison one way or another."

No more hesitation. No more doubt.

Lieutenant Aponi turned to the others, voice sharp and commanding. "Soldiers—gather your things. We have work to do tonight."

Outside, the rain had ceased. The sky above the desert was thick with clouds, but the wind had stilled. The very earth seemed to hold its breath.

A silence before the storm.

Clara spent the night suspended between wakefulness and dreams, her body sinking into the obscenely luxurious bedding while her mind remained taut as a bowstring. The silk sheets—embroidered with delicate cherry blossoms that probably took some poor artisan months to stitch—felt like a mockery against her skin. Even the air smelled wrong here, perfumed with jasmine and oppression.

Every time she closed her eyes, the images came: Tayanita's empty post by the door, Lan's polished lies, the King's crocodile smile. The digital beeps from the adjoining chamber—Aponi running diagnostics, Kateri monitoring communications—formed a reassuring rhythm beneath her anxiety. Her warriors were close. Prepared. Watching.

Dawn came too soon.

The first golden spear of sunlight had barely pierced her window when a firm knock shattered the fragile peace. Clara was already upright, her hand reaching for the dagger under her pillow before Nokomis' voice cut through the door:

"Tayanita's here."

There was something in the way Nokomis said it—not relief, but controlled fury—that sent Clara barefoot across the cold marble floors. She wrenched the door open to find Nokomis' usually composed face tight with barely restrained emotion.

The scene in the receiving room struck like a physical blow.

Tayanita—their fierce, unshakable Tayanita—lay slumped against Aponi's shoulder, her normally vibrant brown skin gone ashen. One eye was swollen shut, her lower lip split, and her fingers... Clara's breath caught. The telltale scorch marks around her fingertips told the story even before Lan's smooth voice cut through the silence:

"Your guard attacked His Majesty's cousin last night." Lan stood flanked by stone-faced servants, her perfect posture unchanged. "Released Firen when he... paid her compliments." A delicate pause. "The young lord only regained consciousness an hour ago. He may suffer memory lost for very long time."

Clara's vision went white at the edges. She guessed exactly what "compliments" meant in BLAND's twisted court.

"And if he hadn't woken up?" Clara's voice dropped to something dangerous and low.

Lan's smile remained intact, but her eyes went flat. "The King awaits you in the Sun Pavilion." She turned with a swirl of embroidered silk, the dismissal absolute.

As the door clicked shut, Tayanita groaned, her one good eye fluttering open. "Bastard... had hands like eels," she slurred through swollen lips. "The guards had masks that seemed to be Firen-proof."

Aponi's grip on Tayanita's shoulder tightened almost imperceptibly—the only outward sign of the storm raging beneath her calm exterior. Her dark eyes, usually so focused and analytical, burned with quiet fury as she met Clara's gaze. "We can't wait any longer," she said, her voice low but vibrating with intensity. "We move. *Today.*"

Clara felt the weight of those words settle over her like armor. Her fingers reached out, gently brushing against Tayanita's scorched fingertips—a fleeting touch that spoke volumes. The blistered skin told a story no words could convey. *This is what mercy looks like in BLAND,* Clara thought bitterly. *Next time, they won't bother with warnings.*

Aponi exhaled sharply through her nose, her mind already calculating routes, risks, contingencies. "The streets empty after nightfall," she said, her fingers unconsciously tracing invisible maps in the air. "We've identified a transport—just need a few more hours to secure it." Her gaze flickered to the window, where the newborn sun painted the sky in deceptive pastels. "The Indian Sea isn't far. Emily's signal should reach us once we're near the border."

Clara straightened, squaring her shoulders as if physically preparing to don the mask she would need to wear. "Well then. I'll meet with the King today," she said, her voice steady despite the anger simmering beneath. She went to shower and put on a local robe she found in the bedroom closet. A deliberate gesture of composure. "Let him think his little demonstration worked. Let him believe we're properly chastened."

The ghost of a smile touched Aponi's lips—not of amusement, but of grim understanding. It was the same expression she wore when staring down impossible odds. "Just come back to us," she said simply.

Clara nodded once, sharply. There were no promises to make—they all knew the risks. But as she turned to prepare for her audience with the King, her resolve hardened into something unbreakable.

She vowed silently. *Tonight, I take my freedom back.*

Just before 6pm, a servant came back to take Clara to see the King.

The throne room had been transformed.

Where once there had been gilded opulence, now a constellation of holographic children, boys and girls, danced across the space, their laughter ringing through the chamber like wind chimes. Clara stood intrigued as a boy of about three years old—his dark curls bouncing—reached out to grab a shimmering butterfly only for it to dissolve into pixels against his small fingers.

"Do you see?" King Malik's voice was warm with pride as he gestured to the display. "No Firen. No fear. Just... happiness."

Clara's chest tightened. The children *did* look happy. A little girl with braids swung higher and higher on a virtual swing, her grin gap-toothed and unburdened. Another pair—boy and girl—built a castle from blocks together, their small hands working in tandem.

"It wasn't easy," the King admitted, stepping closer. The holographic light painted his sharp features in soft pastels, making him look almost boyish. "But imagine a world where boys never have to hide. Where sisters never lose brothers to accidents." His gaze searched hers. "You of all people understand balance—your speech at the Global Fatherhood Initiative moved me deeply. You are different from other ROWFIRs."

Clara's breath hitched. *He knew.*

"Yes, I know. Not just your public addresses, but the private essays. The late-night debates about paternal leave policies. The complaints on for teenage girls unfairly expelled for roughhousing while boys got passes for worse." The King smiled at her reaction. Clara felt like Malik had been stalking her for years.

"You've always seen the injustice of extremes. That's why you're here." He touched a control, and the scene shifted—now showing toddlers napping peacefully in their mother's arms. "No more Purification rituals. No more separations. Just... harmony."

Clara forced her hands to unclench. The vision *was* beautiful. And that's what terrified her.

"Your Majesty," she began carefully, "this is... extraordinary." She let her voice tremble just enough. "But after seeing the girl's institute and what happened to my staff—" A calculated pause. "I need time to process."

To her surprise, the King's eyes softened. "Of course. Thanks for giving me a chance to show you my heart. I'm grateful that you are here." he said with some humble appreciation, as if she'd passed some unspoken test. He tried to reach her hands but Clara stepped back. He smiled warmly and then signal to Lan waiting in the shadows. "Take all the time you need."

As Lan guided her out, Clara focused on keeping her steps measured. Only when they turned the corner did she notice Lan's fingers were clenched just as tightly as hers.

The corridor back to Clara's chambers was lined with portraits of BLAND's past rulers—stern-faced men in gilded frames, their eyes following her like a silent jury. But one image made her pause.

A woman.

Not just any woman—this one was different. Her hands rested gracefully on the arm of a throne, fingers long and unmarred, the nails painted a soft pearl. No gloves. No gold caps. Just... whole.

Lan stopped beside her, her usual poise faltering for half a breath.

"Who is she?" Clara asked, tracing the portrait's edge with her gaze. The woman's smile was serene, her eyes the warm brown of freshly turned earth. She wore a crown of woven jasmine rather than gold.

"Queen Catherine," Lan said, her voice uncharacteristically soft. "His Majesty's true love."

True love? Clara couldn't believe her ears.

"She arrived in BLAND when she was fifteen," Lan continued, stepping closer to the painting. "Born without Firen—a miracle. The people adored her. She planted gardens where there was only sand. Convinced the King to build schools for girls who'd been purified." A pause. "She died bringing their daughter into the world. The child with her."

Clara's chest ached. "Where did she come from?"

Lan's expression shuttered. "No one knows. The King says she appeared one dawn after years of his prayers—a gift from the holy realms." A practiced answer. Too smooth. "This is a picture of her arrival day in miracle. The Queen asked the King to paint and hang it on her last breath."

Clara's eyes were drawn back to the portrait, not to the queen's serene face, but to the gown. It was all wrong. The fashions of BLAND were heavy, brocaded silks that whispered of wealth and weight, but this… this was something else entirely. The fabric seemed to float, a diaphanous layer of ivory chiffon or linen so fine it must have been sheer to the touch. And the embroidery —it wasn't the rigid, geometric patterns she'd seen everywhere else. It was a cascade of delicate, swirling threads in shades of seafoam and silver, ebbing and flowing like the tide over sand.

A memory, sharp and unexpected, lanced through her. Not of a queen, but of a sun-bleached boardwalk. It was the effortless, breezy elegance of a 90s California surf ad, the kind of dress worn by girls with sun-streaked hair, smelling of saltwater and coconut sunscreen. A world away.

Her breath caught. A man shattered by grief, designing a memorial to a woman he loved? He would remember her eyes, her smile, the fall of her hair. He wouldn't conjure the specific, tactile memory of a fabric's weight or the whimsical pattern of its stitch. But a woman stolen from her life? A girl who clung to every fragment of the world she'd lost? She would remember the feel of a dress. This dress. It wasn't a minor discrepancy; it was a scream in a silent room. A detail a forger would never think to get right, and a detail a hostage would never, ever forget.

Three Realizations Struck Clara at Once:

1. The King didn't pray for a queen. He prayed for a solution.
2. Catherine wasn't a gift. She was a prisoner.
3. The daughter who died with her might have been the first test subject.

Lan bowed towards the portrait and then to Clara. "My lady. This way please."

The memory of Catherine's hands—whole, unmarked, *free*—haunted Clara as Lan guided her down the gilded hallway. The late afternoon sun streamed through stained-glass windows, casting fractured rainbows across the marble floors. Then—

A flicker of movement.

From behind an enormous celadon vase, a young woman's face appeared—just for an instant. Early twenties, with sharp cheekbones and the almost same stubborn tilt to her chin as her ROWFIR friend Emily's. But it was the gloves that caught Clara's breath: gold, yes, but unlike any she'd seen in BLAND. These covered *full* fingers, the delicate embroidery at the wrists suggesting they were meant for adornment, not concealment.

"Who was that?" Clara whirled toward Lan.

Lan's smile didn't waver. "My lady?" She gestured to the empty alcove. "There's no one there."

But Clara had seen her. That face—so like Emily's it made her heart pounded—had been real. And the gloves... Why would any woman in BLAND still have intact fingers?

Maybe I missed Emily so much that I'm imagining things. She thought.

The moment Clara crossed the threshold of their quarters; the Buffalo Sisters moved as one.

Kateri barred the door with silent efficiency, her surgeon's fingers testing the lock with clinical precision. Nokomis was already at the vents, her ear pressed to the ornate grille, listening for the telltale hum of surveillance devices. Aponi stood motionless at the center of the room, her dark eyes missing nothing—the rapid pulse at Clara's throat, the way her fingers twisted the fabric of her skirt.

"Please, tell us everything," Kateri's voice low and urgent. No pleasantries. No preamble. War didn't wait for niceties.

Clara did.

She spoke of Catherine's portrait—the way the late queen's ungloved hands rested so casually on the arm of her throne, the foreign cut of her gown that whispered of distant shores. She repeated Lan's hollow explanation about prayers and divine gifts, how the words rang false against her teeth.

And then—the girl.

"She looked like Emily," Clara whispered, pacing the length of the silk rug. "But her gloves… they weren't like the others here. They were decorative." She met Aponi's gaze. "I hope I'm not imaging things."

Aponi's face grim. The unspoken truth hung between them:

Aponi went very still. "That Queen might have been one of the ROWFIRS."

The word landed like a stone in water. Clara had heard whispers of them—women who vanished from their homelands, smuggled across borders to be studied, harvested. "You know about them?"

Aponi exchanged a glance with the others. A silent conversation passed between the sisters, heavy with something Clara couldn't name. Finally, Aponi exhaled. "We know a lot of things. But we will never speak of it to outsiders." Her voice dropped. "We owe Emily our lives."

Clara's pulse spiked. Emily—their mysterious benefactor, the woman who had funded their mission, who had connections in every dark corner of the world. What had she done?

The air in the chamber turned to ice as Kateri stepped forward, her normally steady surgeon's hands betraying the slightest tremor when she pushed her glasses up the bridge of her nose. The lamplight caught the silver streaks in her tightly coiled hair as she spoke words that would unravel everything Clara thought she knew.

"Clara…" Kateri's voice was barely above a whisper, yet it carried the weight of a confession. "You could conceive a daughter with Firen. Emily wanted you to know this… if the time came." A deliberate pause. "She had a child with him—before he took the throne as the crown prince. A little girl who released Firen when was 9. And she was left with Malik living in the Palace."

Clara's breath left her lungs as if she'd been struck.

Emily—hardened warrior Emily, who spoke in gunfire and strategy—had been a mother. A mother who'd given her child to the very monster they were trying to destroy. A daughter who'd considered both powerful and hunted.

"You all knew." Clara's voice was dangerously low as she turned to face the Buffalo Sisters. The betrayal tasted like copper on her tongue. "This whole mission—I'm just bait to retrieve her child. Isn't it?"

Nokomis met her gaze without flinching. "The young woman you passed in the hall today? That's Mia. Emily's deal with the King was simple: she'd ensure your visit if he kept their daughter safe within BLAND's walls." Her fingers absently traced the scar along her jawline. "But Emily never stopped planning to get her back. And you're the key."

A cold realization slithered down Clara's spine. The King didn't just want her compliance—he wanted her womb. A living incubator for his twisted vision of perfected bloodlines. And Emily… Emily had calculated this from the start.

"Tell me," Clara said, her voice sharp enough to draw blood, "if you had to choose between Mia and me at the border, which one stays behind?"

"Emily used to say that a successful lure fishing experience involves catching the fish and keeping the lure." Aponi didn't blink. "We've located Mia's chambers. Tayanita wasn't just assaulted—she'd slipped into the royal quarters to plant a tracker on Mia before the King's cousin interrupted. The 'attack' was cover." She unrolled a silk map across the table, revealing hidden pathways inked in disappearing dye. "Mia meets us tonight at the garden's south gate. There's a smuggler's route by the underground tunnels below the building, and then through the date palms to the servants' quarter. Vehicles wait there."

The sisters moved with practiced efficiency— Aiyana packing medical supplies into hollowed-out scripture books, Winona loading syringes with sedatives disguised as perfume vials. Their silence spoke volumes: this wasn't their first extraction.

Clara strapped her dagger to her thigh, catching her reflection in the ornate mirror. For a heartbeat, three faces stared back: her own fury, the ghost of Catherine's doomed kindness, and the hardened grief Emily must see every morning.

No, she vowed, pressing her palm to the glass until her fingers whitened. *I won't be his experiment or Emily's bargaining chip.*

And when she finally stood before Emily? There would be hell to pay.

CHAPTER 16: MIRAGE AND MIRACLES

With a shared, determined glance, sisters Kaya and Winona had melted into the shadows twenty minutes prior, their mission clear: extract the hidden Princess Mia. The only sound in the guarded corridor had been the soft *hiss* of a sleep-dart and the gentle thud of a slumping body as they worked with silent, efficient grace. Their part, at least, had gone with merciful smoothness.

Meanwhile, a separate group of rebels guided Clara through the palace's underbelly, their path a blur of cold stone and whispered urgency. They emerged into the warm night air just as the other party arrived, a shadow detaching itself to reveal a young woman with Mia's famed silver-blonde hair and wide, frightened eyes.

There was no time for the polite curtsies or formal introductions a meeting of royalty demanded. Clara's greeting was a frantic, shared look across the moonlit path—a silent acknowledgment of their shared danger and strange alliance. Any hope of making an acquaintance would have to wait. The only currency that mattered now was speed. As the group surged forward toward the relative cover of the date palm field, Clara gathered the hem of her borrowed gown in one hand, gripped a sister's offered hand with the other, and ran.

The extraction unfolded with the precision of a well-rehearsed symphony. Kaya moved like liquid shadow through the moonlit date palms, disabling guards with silent efficiency while Winona kept a stabilizing hand on Mia's back, guiding her through the grove with the protective instinct of a mother lion. Tayanita and Aponi flanked Clara, their bodies tense shields against any threat, their eyes scanning the darkness for movement. The humid night air clung to their skin, heavy with the scent of ripe dates and diesel from the stolen pickup truck waiting at the rendezvous point.

When Clara finally collapsed onto the truck's worn bed beside Mia, her muscles trembled with adrenaline. The vehicle lurched forward as Kaya gunned the engine, the tires spitting gravel as they raced toward the open desert. Clara studied the young woman across from her—Emily's daughter—who sat with her spine straight and her gloved hands folded neatly in her lap, her posture eerily reminiscent of the woman who'd sent them on this mission.

"You sit just like your mother," Clara observed, shouting over the wind whipping through the truck bed.

Mia raised an eyebrow, a smirk playing on her lips. "Sounds like you know my mother well."

"Yeah, she totally played me. But I still need to find her ASAP so I can get the full story. The audacity honestly deserves an award." Clara gave a mischievous smile back at Mia. "Please, we're, like, trauma-bonded at this point," Clara laughed.

Mia turned her face toward the fading lights of the palace, her profile sharp against the indigo sky. The wind suddenly quiet down. "The magic revealed itself on my ninth birthday," she began, her voice soft yet clear, carrying the resonance of a memory revisited a thousand times, "It flickered to life right here—" she held up her hand, though the flames were now absent, "—at my fingertips. It paralysed a cousin who had been bullied me for years. I was so proud. But I saw my father's fear. The senior senates gave my father an ultimatum that night. My mother had to choose—stay and face the executioner's blade, guaranteeing my orphanhood… or to flee into the unknown." A pause. "She chose to run, not for her life, but for mine. She chose the promise of a future reunion over the finality of a shared grave."

Clara's throat tightened. Twelve years. Twelve years of Emily carrying that wound while planning this very moment.

"So, you know everything, then," Clara said carefully.

Mia's gold-gloved fingers flexed. "Father believes I'm a gift from the god, even though not in the way he expected. He had a vision that Firen can be controlled, neutralized or even 'purified'." There was no bitterness in her voice, only the quiet acceptance of someone who'd long since made peace with being both treasure and specimen. "He…values me very much. With proper gloves and distance, he reads me political treatises at night. Let me advise on policy."

Clara watched the way Mia's eyes softened when speaking of the king—the conflicted love of a child for a flawed parent. "If he treats you so well, why leave?"

For the first time, Mia's carefully constructed composure shattered. A tremor ran through her gold-gloved hands before she clenched them into fists, the delicate embroidery at her wrists straining with the motion.

 "My world, for years, was four walls and the constant murmur of guards outside my door," she began, her voice a carefully measured monotone that betrayed a pain too deep for hysterics.

"The second night after I got locked in, she came. I'll never forget the sound of the lock turning—not with the usual harsh clang, but with a gentle click. She was there, my mother, a ghost in her own palace. She didn't speak, just pressed a finger to her lips, her eyes blazing with a fear I'd never seen in her before. She took my hand."

For the first time, her steady tone wavered. "We almost made it. But Lan stepped from the shadows of the hallway, and her grip on my hand became a vice. There was no time for words. Just… a single, desperate kiss on my forehead that felt like both a blessing and an apology. And then she was gone, melting into the darkness like a dream."

She finally looked up, her calmness now clearly revealed as the deepest kind of sorrow. "The next morning, they didn't just replace the lock. They installed two. And the number of guards… well, they made certain no one would ever try again."

"Do you think he was trying to protect you?" Clara couldn't help but asking.

"Protect me or his mission?" Mia sounded dreadful.

"When father looks at me," she whispered, her voice fraying at the edges," he doesn't see his daughter. He sees a living laboratory." The words spilled out like blood from a reopened wound." I'm his perfect test subject for Firen-resistant armor. Do you want to know how he 'trains' me?"

A mischievous laugh escaped her lips as the truck jolted over rough terrain, throwing them shoulder-to-shoulder. In the dim light, Clara saw the truth etched in the young woman's face—not just fear, but the hollow-eyed resignation of someone who'd been broken and reassembled too many times.

"He knows I'm terrified of spiders." Mia's breath came faster now. "So, he locks me in a white room—always white, so the blood shows better—with hundreds of them crawling everywhere. Then he sends in soldiers wearing prototype suits. Different versions each time." Her gloved fingers dug into her thighs. "I have to… to defend myself. The suits fail. The men scream. The spiders…One time the suit almost worked. Two hysterical men decided to run towards me. My father initiates the tiny explosive devices installed on their hearts."

A single tear cut through the dust on her cheek, catching the moonlight as it fell." They never clean the room properly between tests. You can still see the outlines where they pressure-washed the last victim off the walls."

The unspoken horror hung between them—that Mia had been forced to kneel in that room, to press her pristine gloves into stains that told stories no daughter should know.

The desert stretched before them, vast and indifferent. Clara looked across the space between them and gazed Mia's hands—the glove warm from her skin, the fingers beneath whole and unbroken. Not a tool. Not a miracle.

"I see you." She looked into Mia's eyes, "Let's bring you to your mother."

The desert night breathed around them, its ancient rhythms pulsing through the cold, thin air. The dunes rose like frozen waves in the moonlight, their crests sharp enough to cut unwary fingers. The truck was stuck and no good use anymore. Mia's breath formed pale ghosts before her lips as she moved. Clara's boots sinking soundlessly into the fine-grained sand.

"Ladies, we have to keep moving before the sunrise. My map says there should be a village just about 3 miles southeast. We shall make it and find another vehicle or some camels at least." Aponi said firmly.

Clara had realized that Aponi was the defector leader among them at this point, Clara was never really the leader but the front of a long-planed scheme.

Beside Clara and Mia, the Buffalo Sisters flowed through the darkness like ink through water - their forms barely disturbing the silvered landscape.

Yet the desert, that fickle mistress, had other plans.

What should have been a straight shot to freedom became instead a cruel maze. The stars above - usually so reliable - seemed to shift and dance behind veils of high cloud. The landmarks they'd memorized during daylight hours had transformed in the darkness, becoming grotesque parodies of themselves. Kateri's compass spun lazily, its needle drunk on some hidden magnetic pull beneath the sands.

Things were just about to look bad. Suddenly-

A flicker of orange in the distance, so faint at first that Clara thought it a trick of her tired eyes. But no - there it was again, a heartbeat of warmth against the endless blue-black night. The scent of burning juniper wood curled through the air, carrying with it whispers of conversation and the faint, musical laughter of young girls.

As they crested the final dune, the camp revealed itself like a scene from some forgotten fairytale. A ring of low tents crouched against the wind; their fabric patched with a hundred different colors - remnants of a dozen different lives stitched together into something new. Solar panels, scavenged from gods-knew-where, tilted toward the sky on makeshift stands, their surfaces dulled by years of sandstorms.

At the center stood a woman who could only be Miranda Wu.

Miranda Wu's gaze cut through the darkness like a lighthouse beam—unwavering, impossible to look away from. The firelight didn't just illuminate her face; it *revealed* her. Gold and shadow sculpted the story of her life into every line and angle: the proud arch of cheekbones that had once turned heads in stadiums, the stubborn set of a jaw that had refused to break under interrogation, the faint scar along her hairline that spoke of a fight won but not unscathed.

Her braid—thick as a ship's mooring rope and threaded with silver like tarnished trophies—slung over one shoulder with the casual elegance of a woman who'd long stopped caring about vanity. The frayed strip of fabric tying it off might have gone unnoticed by most, but Clara recognized the faded stripes of a rugby jersey—the last stubborn thread tethering this warrior to the woman she'd once been before BLAND stole her.

Miranda's hands moved with economical grace as she stirred the pot over the flames, the steam curling around wrists corded with lean muscle. These were hands that had spiked winning tries on muddy pitches, then later wrenched open cargo hold doors to escape captivity. The knuckles—ridged with scars both old and new—glistened with camel fat rendered from their meager supper. Each whitened seam of tissue was a battle flag: *this one from breaking a guard's nose, that one from punching through a window to pull a child from a burning building.*

When she lifted her head, the fire caught in her irises—not just reflecting light, but *challenging* it. Here was a woman who'd stared down armies and sandstorms and the slow erosion of hope… and had simply *outlasted* them all.

Around her, like planets orbiting their sun, clustered a dozen girls in various states of repose. Some slept curled together like puppies, their faces smooth and unlined in sleep. Others sat upright, their watchful eyes tracking Clara's every move. The oldest couldn't have been more than sixteen, the youngest perhaps nine or ten. All shared the same look - not quite fear, not quite hope, but some fierce combination of the two.

"Well now," Miranda said, her voice like whiskey poured over gravel. "Looks like the desert's brought us some strays." She straightened, wiping her hands on her patched trousers, and the firelight caught the network of fine scars that mapped her forearms - each one a story, a battle, a survival.

One of the younger girls - a whip-thin thing with enormous dark eyes - reached out instinctively to clutch at Miranda's sleeve. The older woman didn't shrug her off, just rested a casual hand on the child's shoulder in a gesture so natural it spoke of countless nights of comfort given and received.

"Miranda Wu," she introduced herself, jerking her chin toward Clara. "And this motley crew are my desert roses. Thorny, tough to kill, and prettier than you'd expect in the right light." The girls exchanged glances at that, a few even daring small smiles.

Clara felt something unclench in her chest as she took in the scene. The carefully arranged perimeter of tin-can alarms. The weapons fashioned from scrap metal and sheer ingenuity - a spear made from a tent pole and a kitchen knife, a slingshot with surgical tubing for bands. The way the girls moved around each other with the easy familiarity of a pack, each knowing her place in their fragile ecosystem.

This place wasn't merely a hideout—it was a heartbeat beneath the polished skin of BLAND's so-called purified society, pulsing with quiet defiance. It had taken root like a wildflower pushing through concrete, nourished by sorrow, sharpened by loss, and fed by a ferocity that refused to die. And at its center—its unyielding spine and silent drum—stood Miranda Wu.

Miranda, with shoulders shaped by a lifetime of impact and endurance, and eyes that missed nothing—eyes that had seen too much. Not just a leader. A symbol. A myth in flesh and breath.

Clara's breath caught. The seven Buffalo Sisters, however, simply inclined their heads—*they had expected this meeting all along.* Behind Aponi, Mia hovered like a shadow, her golden gloves glinting in the rising sun.

Miranda's gaze locked onto those gloves. "Royalty," she observed, voice rough as sandpaper. "What brings you to the wilderness, girl?"

Mia lifted her chin. "I'm going to my mother."

"And who might that be?" Miranda's calloused fingers twitched toward the knife at her belt.

"Emily Jones." Mia's voice swelled with pride. "The woman who walked through death many times."

A spark ignited in Miranda's eyes. "Malik's 'unwanted miracle,'" she breathed. "You survived."

Mia startled. "You know of me?"

Miranda's laughter was a dry, broken thing. "I dragged your mother half-dead across this desert when she escaped. Promised

I'd watch for you one day if I see you." She tapped the faded rugby jersey strip tying her braid. "Emily swore she'd send back an army. Looks like she sent her heart instead."

Clara's pulse roared in her ears. "You planned this," she accused Aponi. "Every step—Emily's promise, Miranda's location—you knew."

Aponi's expression remained unreadable. "We adapt. We protect. That is our oath."

Miranda circled Clara, assessing. "And you? What's your role in this drama?"

"Bait," Clara spat. "Delivered to Malik so they could steal his daughter."

Miranda's cracked lips curved. "Good bait is hard to come by. You must have done well." She surveyed their ragged group with the weary amusement of a woman who'd seen too many fools stumble into freedom. "You look like hell warmed over—no offense," she added, nodding to Winona's blood-caked braids.

"Are you followed?" Miranda asked the sisters.

"No yet." Aponi answered.

"Sleep first. War later." Miranda pressed a warm tin cup into Clara's hands with the gravitas of a bartender serving last rites.

The desert night wrapped around them like a heavy cloak as they filed into Miranda's tent—its faded canvas walls patched with memories and resilience. The air inside carried the scent of sun-baked wool and the faint; comforting musk of sage tucked beneath bedrolls.

One by one, the women settled onto the layered rugs—Aponi folding her long limbs with soldier's efficiency, Winona curling protectively around their medical pack, Mia drawing her knees to her chest like a child still learning to take up space. Clara sank onto a pallet near the tent's center, her body aching with the kind of exhaustion that comes not from miles walked, but from truths uncovered.

Only Kaya remained outside.

Through the tent's open flap, Clara caught glimpses of her silhouette—broad-shouldered and unmoving against the star-strewn sky. The desert wind played with the loose strands of Kaya's braid, but the warrior herself might as well have been carved from stone.

"She won't sleep?" Clara murmured to Aponi.

Aponi didn't open her eyes. "Kaya lost a sister to BLAND's night patrols years ago. She doesn't trust the dark."

Clara saw Kateri gave Kaya a pill, probably for energy boost. Kaya's hand drifted to the knife at her belt—a habitual check, like a mother smoothing a child's hair. The moonlight caught the scars crisscrossing her knuckles, each one a story of survival.

Inside the tent, Miranda moved between the sleepers, adjusting blankets with hands that had rocked frightened girls and broken enemy bones with equal tenderness. When she reached Clara, she paused. Miranda pressed an extra blanket into Clara's hands—rough spun but clean, smelling faintly of juniper. She looked at Kaya and then said to Clara quietly, "Rest. Her watch is her gift to you."

As Clara drifted off, the last thing she saw was Kaya's profile—chin lifted, eyes scanning the horizon—keeping vigil over dreams not yet dared to be dreamed.

Clara slept like the dead for the first time in a while, her dreams a fractured reel of memory: her parents swaying to vinyl records in their sunlit living room; a news broadcast of a female astronaut grinning beneath her helmet; the scent of her mother's bergamot tea steeping—

She woke to that same aroma.

"Afternoon," Mia murmured, silhouetted in the tent's opening. Beyond her, Miranda knelt by a fire, stirring a battered pot. The smell—earthy, floral, alive—was unmistakable.

"That's—" Clara's voice cracked.

"Bergamot and desert sage. Emily taught me." Miranda said.

The afternoon sun slanted through the canvas of Miranda's tent, painting golden stripes across the worn rugs where they gathered. Miranda knelt before the smoldering firepit, her scarred hands moving with ceremonial care as she prepared the tea. The battered tin pot—dented from years of use, its surface etched with the ghosts of old flames—sat squarely in the coals, the water within just beginning to sing.

Clara watched as Miranda measured out the leaves: first jasmine, delicate and floral, then a handful of the desert herbs that grew stubbornly in the cracks of BLAND's borders. The blend was familiar in a way that made Clara's eyes wide open—it smelled like her mother's kitchen, like safety, like a home she hadn't seen in too long.

She poured the steaming liquid into chipped ceramic cups, the fragrant steam curling upward in delicate tendrils. "Jasmine for remembrance. Bitterroot for strength."

The first sip burned Clara's tongue, the flavors unfolding in layers—first the floral sweetness, then the earthy punch of herbs that tasted like the desert itself. It was comfort and warning in equal measure, a drink that demanded you pay attention.

Around the fire, calloused hands cradled steaming cups with a tenderness reserved for holy relics. Mia's breath caught as she lifted hers, the fragrant steam swirling before her face like a whispered memory. She closed her eyes, inhaling deeply—for in that fleeting moment, the scent of jasmine and bitterroot carried the ghost of her mother's embrace, the phantom touch of fingers brushing hair from her forehead, the unshakable promise that no darkness lasts forever.

The cup warmed her palms as she drank, the tea's heat spreading through her chest like a long-awaited homecoming.

Outside, Kaya switched with Tayanita who kept watch, her own cup sitting untouched beside her as she scanned the horizon. The desert stretched before them, vast and indifferent, but here, in this sun-warmed hollow with the tea's heat in their hands, they were—for this moment—safe.

Miranda's gaze met Clara's over the rim of her own cup. "Tea's better shared," she said simply. But her eyes said more—that this ritual wasn't just about refreshment, but about trust forged in steam and silence.

"You look like someone from a different world. May I ask how you got here?" Clara asked carefully.

"Thirty years ago," Miranda said peacefully, not looking at any one of them directly, "I was a rising star in women's rugby. Fast. Strong. Unstoppable, they said. I believed it too. Until I met him."

She stirred the fire with a stick, flames flaring gold and orange in her eyes.

"A sports journalist, or so he claimed. He was charming in the way poison can be sweet. Said all the right things. Asked about my training, my team, my future. I thought he saw me."

Miranda paused, eyes flicking to the shadows at the edge of the firelight.

"He did. Just not in the way I imagined."

Her voice hardened, a steel edge beneath the words.

"Turned out he worked for BLAND. His real job was scouting. Cataloging strength. He drugged my wine over dinner—our third date. I woke up in a cargo hold with twelve other women, shackled, stripped of names."

The silence that followed felt like a held breath.

"I broke my chains on the third night after being put into a temporary camp at the edge of Jeru, a camp where they check every smuggled woman physical check before presenting them to the king and aristocracy." she said quietly, as if telling it to the fire instead of the women listening. "Took two guards down with my restraints still on. My hands were bloodied for days. Didn't feel a thing."

She looked up then, her gaze sweeping across the group, landing briefly on each face.

"I've been running ever since. Fighting. Hiding. And collecting them—" She gestured toward the young girls, watching from the shadows, wary but curious. "Some ran after their purification day. Others… they were left behind when their Firen powers sparked early. BLAND doesn't always wait for the ceremony. That's their secret, you know. They call it order. But it's fear. Fear of what we can become before they've trained us to forget it."

Clara felt the weight of those words like stones in her chest. The fire crackled softly, a single ember snapping into the night.

Outside, the wind moved across the desert like a whisper of ghosts. Inside, something ancient and restless stirred—hope, perhaps, or revolution.

And Miranda Wu, with her scarred hands and unbroken spirit, remained at the center of it all.

A woman they tried to silence.

A woman who had become a storm.

One of the girls—no older than fourteen—held up her hands. The fingertips were missing, but the wounds were jagged, uneven. *Self-inflicted.* To escape a worse fate.

Clara's throat tightened.

Miranda's gaze lingered on Mia with an intensity that made the desert air between them hum. It wasn't just curiosity—it was the searching look of a woman comparing ghosts to living flesh, measuring the echoes of history in the curve of a young woman's cheekbone.

"You are a true inspiration for those girls running for freedom." Clara admired Miranda like a spirit leader.

"Freedom always demands its price," Miranda said, her voice roughened by years of whispering across firelight. She turned her scarred palms upward, revealing the old burns along her wrists—the kind left by shackles worn too long. "Some costs break souls before they break chains."

The fire popped as she stirred the embers with a stick, sending up a shower of golden sparks.

"There was a girl," Miranda began, her eyes fixed on the flames. "Seventeen, with eyes like monsoon rains and hands that had never known calluses. They took her the same night they took me—bundled us into that stinking ship's hold with twenty others." A muscle jumped in Miranda's jaw. "She fought differently than the rest of us. Not with nails and teeth, but with words. Reciting poetry to keep our spirits up. Planning escape routes in iambic pentameter."

Clara watched as Miranda's fingers unconsciously traced the faded tattoo on her inner wrist—a tiny rugby ball inked in better days.

"She tried escaping three times," Miranda continued. "The first time, she made it to the docks before they caught her. The second, she nearly reached the desert. The third..." Miranda's throat worked. "The third time, Malik himself intercepted her. Said her purity fascinated him—a girl without Firen in a kingdom drowning in it."

The firelight carved shadows under Miranda's cheekbones as she mimed a crown atop her own head. "Next time I saw her, she was wearing silk instead of shackles. Bumped into her at the marketplace when I was stealing dates to survive. She didn't recognize me at first—not until I showed her this." Miranda tapped her tattoo. "She pressed a purse of gold into my hands and whispered 'Run.' That was the last time I saw Catherine whole."

Mia's gloved hands clenched in her lap. "She died bringing my father's heir into the world. Both of them gone in one night."

Miranda didn't react at first. Then, slowly, she exhaled—a long, measured breath that seemed to release decades of waiting. "Of course she did," she said softly. "Catherine always knew how to make sudden ending."

There was no bitterness in the words. Only the quiet acknowledgment of a truth every woman in that circle understood: in BLAND, queens were temporary.

The firelight caught the gold threads in Mia's gloves as she folded her hands—a gesture too measured for her youth.

"My father never stopped searching for his next queen," she said, her voice carrying the weight of years spent observing court politics. "The noblewomen of BLAND preen and posture, yet his gaze always drifts beyond our borders—toward women like my mother." She adjusted a loose thread on her cuff, the movement deliberate. "I've loved him as daughters do. But I won't excuse his predation dressed up as preference."

The embers crackled between them, casting shadows across Mia's face—the same angles as Emily's, but tempered by Malik's calculating stillness. Her gloves creaked as she clenched her fists—not in anger, but resolve. The kind forged in quiet bedrooms overhearing whispered strategies, in banquet halls where she learned to parse truth from polished lies.

Mia's voice softened as she spoke, her fingers absently tracing the edge of her golden glove—a nervous habit she'd carried since childhood. "My loyalty was never his to claim," she said, the words steady but her eyes shimmering with unspent tears.

The memory surfaced like a long-buried treasure:

That last night with her mother—the hush of the palace corridors, the way Emily had cupped her face with hands that trembled not from fear, but from the sheer force of love. The scent of her mother's hair—wild sage and gun oil—as she pressed their foreheads together.

"Listen to me, my star," Emily had whispered, her breath warm against Mia's cheek. "No matter how far apart we are, no matter

how many walls he builds—I will never stop coming for you. Do you understand? Never."

Then, the most precious gift of all—her mother's fingers weaving through hers, their palms pressed together in the old resistance gesture. A silent vow.

Now, years later beneath the desert sky, Mia uncurled her gloved hand as if she could still feel that promise etched into her skin. "She told me she would bring me to freedom," she murmured. "And here I am."

The fire crackled, bearing witness. Some oaths, it seemed, could outlast even kings.

The firelight painted Miranda's face in chiaroscuro—deep valleys of shadow between sharp planes of amber light. She leaned forward. Her calloused hands spread like a mapmaker revealing forbidden territories. The desert wind stilled, as if holding its breath.

"Every fortress has its flaw," Miranda murmured, her voice roughened by decades of whispering plans in the dark. "Even BLAND's shining walls." Her finger traced an invisible path in the dirt between them. "There's a crack where the old irrigation canals meet the western ramparts. Follow it, and you'll find a smuggler's path that winds down to the Indian Ocean." Her cracked lips parted in a grin that held no joy—only the fierce satisfaction of a woman who'd spent years memorizing her enemy's weaknesses. "From there, the fishing boats run to Singapore under false flags."

One of the younger girls—Linh, with the self-inflicted scars across her fingertips—drew in a sharp breath. Miranda's gaze snapped to her.

"Problem is," she continued, tapping her temple, "BLAND's AI sensors don't sleep. They'll spot heat signatures larger than a desert hare."

Aponi didn't hesitate. Her hands moved to the hidden

compartment of her tactical vest, retrieving a device no larger than a deck of cards. It gleamed dully in the fire light; its surface etched with circuitry that seemed to shift when viewed from different angles.

"EM bubble generator," she said, her fingers dancing across the interface. Tiny LEDs blinked to life, casting her face in eerie blue. "Cancels all active scanning within a 30-meter radius. Makes us…" She glanced at the wide-eyed girls circling the fire. "Invisible."

A hush fell over the group as Aponi activated the device, its faint blue glow illuminating faces that had known too many nights without hope. The air itself seemed to vibrate with possibility— that fragile, precious thing they'd all learned to ration like water.

Linh reached out first, her damaged fingertips—each missing joint a story of defiance—hovering just above the blinking machine. The light played over her scars, turning the ridges silver. Her breath caught in a way Clara recognized; it was the sound of someone who'd stopped daring to imagine freedom long ago, only to find it suddenly within reach.

"It's real," Linh whispered, more to herself than the others. The words carried the weight of a prayer.

They departed under a sky streaked with violet and amber, the last reluctant gift of a desert that had been both prison and protector. Miranda and two other older girls each carried a large backpack. The packs contain food ration bars that Miranda and her team stole from a BLAND military base two years ago. Miranda moved at the head of their ragged column, her posture straight despite the weight of her pack, her dark eyes scanning the terrain with the precision of a woman who'd spent years memorizing every shadow and dune.

A nervous, silent procession of girls moved through the twilight, their soft footfalls the only sound in the vast emptiness. They clung to each other in pairs, their youth palpable in the quick, birdlike glances they cast into the shadows.

But Mia walked alone at their heart, a portrait of resolve. Upon her hands, she still wore gloves—not of silk, or gold thread, unlike her usual ones in the palace. However, she carried her gold gloves and coins in her pockets.

Let them see the gold first, she thought, her chin lifted not in arrogance, but in the unwavering dignity of her bloodline. *Let them hesitate for one second—long enough to recognize the symbol, to question their orders. One second of respect could be all the time these children need to run.*

Every step was a gamble. The gloves were a shield forged from her own gilded cage, and tonight, she would use her captivity to buy their freedom.

Clara brought up the rear, her body thrumming with the awareness of being watched—not by living eyes, but by the desert itself. The wind sighed through the rocks, carrying the scent of sage and something sharper, like ozone before a storm.

They walked all night under the milky way.

And, so as the next three nights.

Exhaustion dictated their rhythm, forcing them to make camp in the scant shade during the blistering daylight hours. Their meals were a silent, utilitarian affair: tearing open BLAND ration packs that tasted of dust and preservation, and sipping warm, vaguely gritty water that had been hurriedly filtered through cloth. It was a testament to their resolve—that even in this stark reality, they took the time to care for their bodies, to share what little they had, and to find a sliver of rest before the peril of the night's journey began again.

The third dawn came softly, as if hesitant to disturb their fragile procession.

First, a blush of rose along the eastern horizon, delicate as the inside of a seashell. Then gold spilling slow as honey across the indigo expanse, the colors swirling together like ink in water. By the time they reached the riverbank, the sky had lightened to the pale, fragile blue of a robin's egg—that fleeting shade that exists only in the hour between darkness and day.

The air started to get thicker.

A river stretched before them, its surface obscured by tendrils of mist that rose like ghosts from the water. The air hung thick with moisture, coating their skin and clothes, the chill of it a shock after the desert's dry embrace. Somewhere beyond that curtain of fog lay freedom, safety, answers.

Clara turned for one last look at the land behind them. The desert stood silent, its dunes gilded by the newborn light, already erasing their footprints from the sand.

And what a river it was.

The Jaruun sprawled before them, broad and indolent, its currents moving with the drowsy rhythm of a beast barely roused from sleep. The mist clung to its surface in spectral tendrils, parting occasionally to reveal water the color of tarnished silver.

Clara's breath caught. There, half-submerged in the reeds like a discarded dream, crouched the remains of a dock. Its pilings leaned drunkenly against the current, their wood weathered to bone-gray. Nets hung in tattered shrouds from rusted cleats, swaying gently in the dawn breeze.

"Looks like the last fisherman has left this dock for long time." Miranda said, her voice barely heard by Aponi over the river's whisper. "When BLAND's sensors made the waters too dangerous." She nodded to the eastern bank where the patrol boats are parked showing its relentless push against civilization. "The Indian Ocean is there. Just beyond the mist."

Aponi's device hummed to life in her palm, its LEDs pulsing like a heartbeat.

"Time to be ghosts," she said.

The mist parted before them like a curtain drawing back on a new act. As the first true light of dawn gilded the river's surface, they stepped forward—not as desperate fugitives scrambling for freedom, but as deliberate shadows slipping through the seams of BLAND's carefully constructed reality. The morning air tasted of wet reeds and diesel, thick with promise.

And there she was.

Tethered to the rotting dock like an afterthought, a patrol boat rocked gently in the pewter-colored water. Sun-bleached paint curled away from her hull in long, peeling strips, revealing decades of hasty repairs beneath—streaks of rust like old scars, patches of mismatched metal where bullets had once torn through. Yet she sat low and steady in the water, a veteran of countless border runs. The engine compartment hummed faintly, a sleeping beast still loyal to its purpose despite years of neglect.

"Seems Malik owes us one last parting gift," Aponi murmured, her voice rough as wind over sandstone. The half-smile that curved her lips didn't reach her eyes—those remained sharp, assessing. She gestured to Kaya, and the two moved in synchronized silence, shadows against the growing light.

The patrol soldiers never stood a chance.

Aponi's strike was clinical—a tap on the pressure point behind the ear, a gentle lowering of the unconscious body to the deck. Kaya handled the other two with the quiet efficiency of someone who'd done this dance before, her hands steady as she relieved them of weapons and comm units. The entire operation took less than thirty seconds, the only sound the lap of water against the hull and the distant cry of a heron.

Then came the hacking of the control panel. Without breaking stride, Kaya reached into her side pocket. Her fingers, knowing exactly what to find, closed around the sleek, cool metal of her decoding device. In one fluid, practiced motion, she pulled it out and activated it, the screen flaring to life with a soft blue glow. It was the kind of effortless grace that came from having done something not a million times, but enough to make it a part of her very muscle memory. Her fingers flew across the keypad, bypassing security protocols with the ease of someone who spoke the language of machines as fluently as her native tongue. The panel flickered, spat static, then glowed green.

"Welcome aboard, ladies," Kaya whispered.

One by one, they stepped onto the deck. Clara felt the subtle shift beneath her feet—the living vibration of machinery, the buoyant resistance of water. The engine coughed once, twice, then caught with a stuttering growl that shattered the morning's fragile silence. The sound vibrated up through Clara's boots, settling in her bones like a battle cry.

As the boat carved through the water, Clara turned for one last look at BLAND—its gilded walls glowing in the dawn light like a gilded cage. The empty dock shrank behind them, its broken pilings jutting from the water like skeletal fingers, as if trying to drag them back. For a heartbeat, she swore she saw them—shimmering figures lining the shore, the ghosts of those who'd tried to escape before. Women who had run. Women who had failed.

Then the mist rolled in, thick and forgiving, swallowing BLAND whole.

When Clara turned away, it was with the slow unclenching of a fist she hadn't realized she'd been holding. The land became a smudge on the horizon, its glittering spires now just a mirage of marble and lies. *Tombstones*, she thought. Every polished facade marking where someone's daughter had been buried alive.

Then—

"Jackpot!"

Aiyana's voice shattered the silence like a stone through glass. She was elbow-deep in a storage compartment, her braids swinging as she emerged victorious, a water canister held aloft. Sunlight caught the droplets sloshing inside, turning each one into a liquid diamond.

"Look at this!" she shook two big canisters so the water danced. "Enough to drown in—well, not literally," she amended with a grin, "but four days' worth, easy!"

The sound that escaped Clara's lips was half laugh, half sob. Around her, the others surged forward, their cracked lips stretching into smiles as they crowded around Aiyana, their fingers brushing the precious cargo with something like reverence.

Her grin widened as she rummaged deeper, emerging with two fishing rods and a crabbing net clutched in her fists. "And guess what else these geniuses left lying around? Dinner delivery service!" She waggled the rods, the lines unraveling in a silvery cascade. "Who's ready to eat something that didn't come shrink-wrapped in a BLAND ration pack?"

The girls whooped, their cracked lips stretching into smiles for the first time in days. Even the ever-stoic Miranda chuckled, shaking her head. "Leave it to you to sound excited about manual labor."

"Darling," Aiyana shot back, already rigging the line with practiced fingers, "after three days of that recycled desert swill, I'd wrestle a shark barehanded for a proper meal." People laughed.

The boat glided effortlessly across the water, its steady engine humming in harmony with the gentle waves. Sunlight danced on the surface, painting ripples of gold as the breeze carried the fresh, salty scent of the sea.

The passengers sat in comfortable silence, not out of unease, but from a quiet mutual respect. Supplies were limited—food carefully portioned, water measured with mindful precision—and so they moved with intention, conserving energy for the journey ahead.

Above them, the sky stretched clear and endless, the sun warm but not harsh. The ocean remained calm, as if nature itself had paused to grant them safe passage. There was a serenity in the air, a sense of being exactly where they were meant to be.

For now, the world was soft, and the sea carried them forward like an old friend.

Four days later, the boat creaked under the relentless sun, its metal deck burning hot enough to blister skin. Clara ran her tongue over cracked lips, tasting blood. The last canteen had run dry hours ago, passed between parched mouths like a sacred relic. Even Miranda—whose desert-hardened resilience usually outlasted them all—leaned heavily against the railing, her eyes scanning the endless horizon with growing unease.

Clara stumbled into the control room, where Kaya's fingers flew over the navigation panel. The dim screens cast ghostly light over her sweat-streaked face.

"Are we nearing any safe land?" Clara rasped.

Kaya didn't look up. "We passed BLAND's signal blackout two days ago. Aponi already pulsed our coordinates to Emily." A faint beep sounded—a confirmation. "Rescue should be on route."

Clara exhaled, whispering to the stale air, "Come on, Emily. Don't make me regret calling you sister."

An hours later, a shout rang out from the deck.

The girls—sunburned, exhausted—staggered to their feet as a sleek naval vessel cut through the waves toward them. Its hull gleamed like a promise under the setting sun.

"Emily found us," Aponi announced, her voice thick with relief.

All eyes were locked on the vessel, a dark shape against the blazing sky that grew steadily, transforming from a forgotten hope into a tangible promise.

It was more than excitement that swelled in their chests—it was a dizzying wave of relief so profound it stole their breath. Rough, calloused hands reached for each other, fingers lacing together in a silent pact of shared survival. Tears, previously held back by sheer will, now traced clean paths through the dust on their cheeks. They stood together, hearts pounding in a unified rhythm of gratitude and awe, watching their salvation draw near. No words were needed; the language of their hope was written in every trembling smile and every squeezed hand.

But as they boarded, something felt... *off*.

The ship's crew moved with military precision, distributing water bottles and protein bars with practiced efficiency. Yet Emily was nowhere in sight. Instead, a towering woman with a lightning-shaped scar under her left eye stepped forward—Captain Siku Mato, her posture radiating quiet authority.

"Welcome aboard," she said, her voice deep and steady. "President Jennifer sent me to ensure your safe return. The administration is eager to celebrate your bravery."

Aponi's grip tightened on her canteen. "The President? Not Emily?"

Siku's expression remained unreadable. "That's a question for President Jennifer herself. She's waiting for you."

Mia pushed forward, her golden gloves catching the light. "Is my mother safe?"

"She is," Siku assured, her tone softening. "You'll see her soon."

Clara's instincts prickled. *Why would the President intervene in a rogue op Emily orchestrated?* But exhaustion won out. For now, survival was enough.

Clara woke to the rich, comforting aroma of coffee—real coffee, not the burnt acorn brew they'd survived on for days. Sunlight streamed through the porthole, painting warm stripes across the crisp linen sheets. For the first time in weeks, her body felt *safe*.

But as she sipped from the steaming mug, her mind churned. *What game is the President playing? And where the hell is*

Emily?

Somewhere beyond these steel walls, answers waited.

But for now—just for now—she let the coffee's warmth seep into her bones, savoring the simple luxury of being *found*.

CHAPTER 17: SHADOW OF A QUEEN

Mia got her own private room on the Navy vessel, where everyone else were bunked together.

Quite the royal privilege, Clara thought.

The next night, Captain Siku Mato hosted a welcome back party on the ship for all the returning ladies. The deck of the ship was bathed in silver moonlight, the ocean stretching endlessly under a sky thick with stars. Clara leaned against the railing, letting the cool breeze soothe the warmth of wine in her veins. The party inside was still alive with laughter and music, but out here, the world felt quieter. More honest.

That's when she saw Mia again.

The girl stood alone, her silhouette framed by the night, her fingers tracing the edge of a pendant around her neck—a habit Clara had noticed before.

"Couldn't handle the crowd either?" Clara asked, stepping beside her.

Mia didn't turn. "Just thinking."

Clara hesitated, then softened. "I hope you find your mother safe when we arrive."

A pause. Then, bitterly: "You wouldn't say that if you knew the whole story."

Clara frowned. "What do you mean?"

Mia didn't respond.

"I get that you're feeling unsettling. It's never easy to have a mother-daughter reunion after many years of separation."

Mia's grip tightened on the railing.

"You don't understand." Mia sighed, "Love is tough, but politics is tougher."

At this point, Clara is more intrigued by Mia than ever.

Mia sighed again, "Let me tell you a love story first."

And then, under the indifferent stars, Mia began to unravel the past.

Once, Malik had been a prince with gentle hands and a heart too tender for the throne.

At sixteen, he watched his twin brother die in battle—burned alive by Firen. That day, fear carved itself into his bones. Fear of the power that lived inside women. Fear of becoming like his father, who ruled with cruelty, who made his mother weep over severed fingers.

Then, at twenty, he met her.

Even though she arrived unwillingly by smuggler's boat. Emily was fire wrapped in flesh—sharp-tongued, bold, unafraid to shove him against a palace wall and demand, "When will men like you stop pretending you don't see the chains around everyone?"

And Malik—soft-hearted, hopeful Malik—loved her for it.

He allowed her to enjoy many privileges on his land. He loved her when she stormed council meetings, when she spat at traditions, when she made him believe, for the first time, that a king could be more than a figurehead. That he could be more.

But the crown is heavy.

Marriage changed them.

Malik became king. Emily became a queen who refused to kneel.

At first, he fought for her. But the nobles whispered. The generals threatened. The Mother Goddess warned of chaos.

And Malik—who still dreamed of his mother's tears—remembered the cost of rebellion.

"If I push too hard, they'll replace me," he confessed one night, hollow-eyed. "And then what happens to you? To our daughter?"

Emily had stared at him, betrayal sharp in her throat. "You'd rather let them win?"

But it wasn't about winning. It was about surviving.

So, he compromised. He allowed the Purification Laws. He buried his guilt in the hope that, someday, science could undo what tradition had wrought.

And Emily?

Emily realized the palace wasn't a throne room.

It was a gilded cage.

Mia's voice wavered. "She left because she had to. Not because she didn't love me."

Clara's chest ached. "But you were just a child—"

"And I would've been burned alive together with her if she stayed." Mia turned, her eyes glistening. "The nobles would not stop pressure my father and his throne until she is gone. And my father promised the nobles that he would make my mother disappear, as long as they keep me intact. She left so I could have a life outside their games."

The truth hung between them, raw and aching.

Some love stories don't end with a kiss.

Some end with a queen walking away, her heart in pieces, because life of a child was the only gift left to give.

Clara studied Mia—really studied her—for the first time. The way the moonlight caught the sharpness of her gaze, the way her fingers didn't fidget, the way she spoke with a weight no sixteen-year-old should carry.

"Sounds like your father really talks about everything with you," Clara said, trying to mask the unease creeping up her spine.

Mia smiled, slow and knowing. "Yes. He also told me I'm the only reason Jennifer hasn't nuked BLAND off the map."

Clara's wineglass froze halfway to her lips. "Jennifer? As in—the president?" The name rolled off Mia's tongue like a childhood friend, not the most powerful woman in the world.

"She and my father have a direct line. Sometimes, he lets me sit in on their calls." A flicker of pride—or was it something darker?—passed over Mia's face.

Clara's pulse quickened. "Wait. Back up. How are you the reason BLAND still exists?" She leaned in, the salt-stung wind suddenly too cold. "Are you some kind of diplomat?"

Mia's grin faded. For the first time, hesitation. She bit her lip, then turned her face toward the blackened horizon.

"Not a diplomat," she said softly. "Collateral."

The word hung between them, sharp as a blade.

Clara's breath hitched. "What do you mean, collateral?"

Mia didn't blink. "Malik knows Jennifer won't drop a bomb if I'm still inside the blast radius. Just like I know she'd never hurt my mother." Her voice was ice. "Mutual destruction only works if someone's left to mourn the pieces."

Clara's stomach dropped. "But—why would Jennifer care about —"

"Because she is my aunt." Mia finally turned, her smile slicing through the night. "Emily's younger sister."

Silence.

Clara's glass slipped from her fingers, shattering on the deck. The sound was too loud, too violent for the quiet sea.

Clara swallowed her saliva and some air. "You've got to be

kidding me." Her voice shook. "This whole time—your parents and your aunt—they used you? As a—a bargaining chip?"

Mia's laugh was hollow. "Welcome to politics, Clara. The first rule? Never underestimate a woman who's spent her life playing the long game."

And just like that, Clara realized—

She wasn't standing across from a child.

She was standing in the shadow of a queen.

"Goodnight, Clara." Her voice was softer now, the polished edge of their earlier conversation worn down to something almost fragile. "Tomorrow is… another interesting day."

The way she said it—not with excitement, but with the quiet resignation of someone who had learned too young that "interesting" often meant dangerous—sent an unexpected pang through Clara's chest. Mia held her gaze a heartbeat longer than necessary, as if trying to convey something words couldn't capture. Then, with a small, tired smile that didn't reach her eyes, she turned and disappeared into the noise and light.

Alone again, Clara became acutely aware of the vast, indifferent darkness pressing in around her. The wind carried the scent of salt and something colder—the metallic tang of distant storms. She wrapped her arms around herself, but the chill had settled deeper than the night air could account for.

Below her feet, the ship cut through black water, each wave whispering against the hull like secrets against skin. Somewhere ahead, beyond the curve of the horizon, tomorrow waited—heavy with unspoken truths and the weight of Mia's knowing smile. Clara exhaled slowly, watching her breath mist in the air before vanishing.

Another interesting day.

The words hung between her and the stars, neither promise nor warning, but something far more unsettling:

An invitation.

The next morning, ahead, across the slow waters and the breath of morning mist, rose the skyline of Singapore. It emerged like a fabled city—part real, part dream—its towers bathed in the soft gold of sunrise. There was something honest in its silhouette, something unscripted. Clara blinked against the light, unsure if it was the sun or hope stinging her eyes.

A small hand tugged at her sleeve.

It was the girl with the jagged fingers—the one who never spoke above a whisper, who had flinched the first time Clara had tried to brush her hair. Her voice now was small but clear, trembling with something between fear and wonder.

"Is it true?" she asked, barely more than breath. "Out there… girls get to keep their hands the way it is?"

Clara looked down at her. Looked at the damage BLAND had done—fingers, twisted and gone, tendons scarred like burnt lace. She took the girl's hand gently in hers, cradling what was left with reverence, not pity. Her own voice came out soft and sure.

"Yes," she said. "Out there, they do."

And as the ship moved forward into the bay, parting the water with the grace of deliverance, Clara felt something shift inside her—something fragile but bright. A smile broke across her face, hesitant, then certain. It was the kind of smile that hadn't touched her lips in days—maybe years. Not the smile of survival, but of beginning.

"Whatever is ahead. I'm coming for it." Clara murmured.

Story to be continued

Follow us on YouTube: www.youtube.com/@firenworld

Manufactured by Amazon.ca
Acheson, AB